"I will sacrifice anything and everything to destroy our Goddess's enemies."

Sanctina
A young female hero known as the Saint.

The
DIRTY
WAY to DESTROY the GODDESS'S
HEROES

2

No Reply.
It's Just a Saint.

"You're the one who taught this innocent body to crave such naughty things."

Celes

A maid ranked number two most magically powerful in the Demon King's castle. She has a mercilessly sharp tongue.

"The first time I saw you, I thought you were a coolheaded bombshell. Oh, why'd you have to turn out like this...?"

"Well, I thought the skewers were really yummy."

Shinichi Sotoyama
An abnormally brave high school student and the advisor for the Blue Demon King.

Arian
A bright and cheerful young hero. She's become a little klutzy now that she's blinded by love.

The DIRTY WAY to DESTROY the GODDESS'S HEROES

No Reply. It's Just a Saint.

2

SAKUMA SASAKI

Illustration by **ASAGI TOSAKA**

YEN ON

New York

The Dirty Way to Destroy the Goddess's Heroes
Sakuma Sasaki

Translation by Jordan Taylor
Cover art by Asagi Tosaka

MEGAMI NO YUSHA WO TAOSU GESU NA HOHO Vol. 2 HENJI GA NAI, TADA NO SEIJO NO YODA.
©Sakuma Sasaki 2017
First published in Japan in 2017 by KADOKAWA CORPORATION, Tokyo.
English translation rights arranged with KADOKAWA CORPORATION, Tokyo through TUTTLE-MORI
AGENCY, INC., Tokyo.

English translation © 2019 by Yen Press, LLC

Yen On
150 West 30th Street, 19th Floor
New York, NY 10001

Visit us at yenpress.com
facebook.com/yenpress
twitter.com/yenpress
yenpress.tumblr.com
instagram.com/yenpress

First Yen On Edition: November 2019

Yen On is an imprint of Yen Press, LLC.
The Yen On name and logo are trademarks of Yen Press, LLC.

Library of Congress Cataloging-in-Publication Data
Names: Sasaki, Sakuma (Novelist), author. | Tosaka, Asagi, illustrator. |
Taylor, Jordan (Translator), translator.
Title: No reply. It's just a saint. / Sakuma Sasaki ; illustration by Asagi Tosaka ;
translation by Jordan Taylor.
Other titles: Henji ga nai, tada no seijo no yoda. English
Description: New York, NY : Yen On, 2019.
Identifiers: LCCN 2019011081 | ISBN 9781975357115 (v. 1 : pbk.) |
ISBN 9781975357139 (v. 2 : pbk.)
Classification: LCC PL875.5.A76 O613 2019 | DDC 895.63/6—dc23
LC record available at https://lccn.loc.gov/2019011081

ISBNs: 978-1-9753-5713-9 (paperback)
978-1-9753-5714-6 (ebook)

10 9 8 7 6 5 4 3 2 1

LSC-C

Printed in the United States of America

The DIRTY

WAY to DESTROY the GODDESS'S
HEROES

No Reply.
It's Just
a Saint.

Illustration by Asagi Tosaka

Prologue

The world of Obum comprised three large continents. Uropeh was one of them.

Smack in the middle of it was the one and only Holy City, built on the exact location that the Divine Goddess Elazonia first descended in Obum, and it sprawled across a large section of the continent. However, the massive city wasn't ruled by a king or an emperor.

There was only one group of people fit to govern it: the Holy See, the top dogs of a religious organization that now boasted over ten million devotees.

Carved out of the whitest marble and gleaming in the sunlight, the Archbasilica stood as the transmuted form of the Holy See's Divine Goddess. Its sight even spurred nonbelievers to bow their heads in prayer.

In the very back corners of this holy building, though, a group was finishing up a shady trial.

"We will now administer your punishment."

With their backs turned to a statue of the original Goddess, which the first pope had painstakingly carved, four elders spoke with pomp and circumstance.

They were cardinals of the church, charged with overseeing the Holy See in place of the ill pope. As their icy stares bore straight into the accused, the young man in his early thirties trembled slightly.

This was Bishop Hube, who'd had Boar Kingdom wrapped around his little finger.

"You have been accused of committing sexual violence against the hero Arian, forcing her to leave your kingdom. Your actions incited our Goddess's anger, which destroyed the Cathedral of Boar Kingdom. I must say, these crimes are difficult to overlook."

"Please wait. As I've said—," Hube started, having desperately tried excuse after excuse.

But the holy warrior behind him thrust the butt of his spear into Hube's back, silencing him. With pity and contempt, the four cardinals observed this pathetic sight before handing down his sentence with cool indifference.

"For his crimes, the accused will be stripped of his title as bishop and sentenced to ten years of imprisonment in the dungeon."

"No…," whimpered Hube, despondent. The blood drained from his face and left it ashen.

He wasn't just losing his status and honor, which he'd worked so hard to attain as a loyal follower of the Goddess. He was losing his future, trapped in a cold, dark cell.

"Mercy! Please have mercy!" he pleaded over the warrior's brutal blows to his back.

But the cardinals' responses were colder than a river in the middle of winter.

"We've considered your long-standing history and service to the church for your sentence. We have exhibited more than enough mercy," said the first cardinal.

"Indeed. It was a big blow to the church to lose a promising hero," continued the second. "But more than that, we cannot forgive you for destroying a cathedral."

"Or for making the people of Boar Kingdom lose faith in the church," added the third.

"It is unfortunate," concluded the fourth. "But we must punish you for your deeds to set an example."

Their faces mirrored their sentiments and seemed very regretful. In their hearts, however, they had been envious of the young bishop, who'd risen through the ranks so quickly.

But even without these underlying motives, it was true that Hube's crimes had tarnished the reputation of the church, and they could not be taken lightly.

"I suggest you offer prayers to our Goddess Elazonia and repent for your crimes in your cell."

"Please listen to me! This was all carried out by that evil boy! I've done nothing wrong!" Hube begged.

"…That's enough. Take him away."

"Yes, sir!"

As Hube continued to struggle and flail, two holy warriors flanked him, grabbing him by his arms and trying to drag him out of the room.

"Damn you… You filthy heretiiiiiiiiics—!" he screeched.

Was he addressing the black-haired boy who'd framed him or the cardinals who'd sentenced him? We'll never know.

The heavy doors slammed shut behind them, and the trial was officially over.

"My, my, kids these days," lamented the first cardinal. "It troubles me that they have no self-control."

"Agreed. If he can't even admit to his own failures, he never had a future anyway," mused the second.

"He was too blessed and too gifted to ever experience failure. It's just the way it is," placated the third.

"We have already handed down his sentence," spoke the fourth. "It would be cruel to blame him any further."

The four elders let out tired sighs, but they immediately straightened up and settled back into the stern expressions of cardinals.

"But we cannot dismiss the evil that's cropped up in a valley near Boar Kingdom," began the first.

"Agreed," continued the second. "If we leave these demons unattended, especially after they've wronged our Goddess, it will destroy our reputation."

"That said," interjected the third, "I've heard that Arian was barely able to leave a scratch on the so-called Blue Demon King before she fled for her life."

"Seeing that she defeated the massive black wolf—no match for *twenty* of our holy warriors—if this opponent forced her to run... Well, I can't even imagine how terrifying he is." The fourth shivered.

The cardinals might have been old, but they weren't any run of the mill magic users. All of them had received the Goddess's blessing, making them undying heroes—veterans of defeating monsters. This was why they could completely understand the extent of the Blue Demon King's power, which caused a cold sweat to spring to their cheeks.

"It might be possible to defeat him," postulated the first, "if we deploy the entire force of the church."

"Agreed," replied the second. "But that course of action would not be wise."

"If we left our Holy City unprotected, we would be welcoming disaster and danger with open arms," contested the third. "I think that goes without saying."

"And as unfortunate as it is, one can hardly say we're a united front," stated the fourth.

At first glance, the cardinals' eyes all rested serenely, but a razor-sharp glint had just flashed through them as they thought the same thing.

The pope was at the mercy of a disease that was incurable, even with magic: His body was succumbing to old age, and he would soon be called to heaven's gates. On that occasion, one of the four cardinals would be selected to succeed him and become the highest authority in the church, governing over ten million devotees. It would basically make them the leader of the entire continent.

Each of the candidates had their own motivations to become pope, whether it was faith, fame, or something else. Even though their motives were different, they were all intent on rising up in the church. After all, they'd all managed to claw their way up to cardinal one way or another.

This was why sparks flew under the surface of all their interactions. In this heated competition for the next papal appointment, they were all looking for a leg up. To them, the appearance of the Blue Demon King posed a wonderful opportunity to rise to the occasion—or a dangerous mire into which any of them could sink.

Their enemy was an all-powerful demon that had managed to fend off a hero, known as Red for the color of her hair. If one of them could succeed in making the demon surrender and spreading the Goddess's grace, that candidate would be appointed as the new pope.

But if they failed, they would risk losing their power—or worse, end up like ex-bishop Hube. Even if they didn't fail, they ran the risk of other candidates stealing their followers and whittling away their support if they were away from the Holy City for too long.

This problem with the demons was like a chestnut roasting in a fire: It was sweet and tantalizing, but it could burn a careless hand trying to fish it out.

"For now," started the first, "we should all accept that we cannot directly handle this issue."

"Agreed," spoke the second. "We might cause unnecessary unrest if we act without caution."

"That said," mused the third, "do we have any heroes who can win against Arian?"

"Even if they lack certain skills, we might stand a chance if we make them form a team. What do you think?" asked the fourth.

The other three cardinals grimaced at the suggestion made by the only female cardinal in the group.

"It's not a bad idea," said the first. "But the more powerful the hero, the more difficult their personality, which means they'll only work with their favored few..."

"Agreed," asserted the second. "That is why we were so eager about Arian's potential, especially because she was unusually honest and pure."

"Bishop Hube really did a number on us," said the third.

As they exchanged their superficially glum commentary, they were partially relieved: Hube was not a subordinate to any of them. He had been trying to pull himself up to cardinal. From the perspectives of the papal candidates, Arian was seeing too much success under his care.

With Hube out of the picture, Arian would make a wonderful pawn to whoever managed to snag her—not that she was anywhere to be found.

"Well, we cannot rely on an absentee. Which is why I propose we send Sanctina."

"Hmm…"

This was Cronklum's idea. He was the eldest and the closest to being appointed as the next pope among them. The other three murmured "As we expected" in response.

"So you intend to dispatch your favorite disciple," confirmed the second, "Saint Sanctina."

"With our holy warriors at her side, she may be able to destroy the Demon King," said the third, "once and for all."

"Well then, we shall go ahead with that," concluded the fourth.

They approved Cronklum's proposal with surprising speed.

As things were, he was in line to become the next pope, so nothing would change if he succeeded. But if he were to fail his mission, it would put a black mark on his record.

At the same time, they knew they would face retribution and backlash if they resisted his plan, especially if he was appointed as the next pope.

Cronklum probably knew they would approve his proposal for these very reasons, and he smiled and nodded before calling to someone outside of the room.

"I'm assuming you all agree with my plan. Sanctina, please come in."

"Yes, Your Eminence," replied a charmingly high voice, as clear as a bell.

A young girl slipped through the doors.

With porcelain skin, she had long platinum-blond locks reminiscent of the sun. In fact, Saint Sanctina was so beautiful that some said she was a living replica of the Goddess herself.

"Your Eminences, I am honored to be graced with your presence," said Sanctina, delicately gathering the skirt of her pure-white robe and giving a graceful curtsy.

All the cardinals except Cronklum cooed with admiration in spite of themselves.

"You've grown even more beautiful, Miss Sanctina."

"And it seems you've polished your magical powers."

Underneath it all, they wryly thought: *I'd expect nothing less from Cronklum's perfect little doll.* Not that any of them voiced their true feelings or showed any hint of it on their faces.

They were thinking about how Sanctina was a product of his labor and money.

Cronklum had searched far and wide to find attractive magic users—men and women—and paid them to have babies. He then took these children and exposed them to magic from an early age, increasing their magical capacities.

Of course, he didn't forget to indoctrinate them with the teaching of the Goddess. With faith drilled deep into their brains, they grew up to become his faithful pawns. The most magically gifted among them was Saint Sanctina, an undying hero.

It can't be said that brainwashing and eugenics are within the realm of sanity, but sanity has very little to do with faith, you know.

"Sanctina, you are to lead the team and destroy the demons in Dog Valley."

"Yes, Your Eminence. I will sacrifice anything and everything to destroy our Goddess's enemies," replied Sanctina to Cronklum's command.

After all, he was a cardinal—and the man who'd raised her.

She accepted her duties without fear, wearing a serene smile that was befitting of a saint. It glittered and reflected her unwavering belief in the love and justice of the Goddess Elazonia.

Chapter 1
A Day in the Life of Demons

Along the banks of a flowing river, farming villages of all shapes and sizes dotted far and wide between Dog Valley and Boar Kingdom. In one such town, Potato Village, a chief frowned, puzzled, as he scanned the faces of his peculiar customers.

"Twenty boxes worth of potatoes, one head of livestock, and some olive oil... Are you sure you want to give me thirty gold coins for *that*?"

"Yes, of course," laughed a merchant, Manju, as he nodded.

He was a man of average height and average build with no distinguishing features. As promised, he handed the gold over to the village chief.

The chief's hands were weighed down by the heavy coins, forcing him to stagger. Even though he governed a village of a hundred residents, this was the first time he'd ever held such a large amount of cash in his hands at once.

"You're really giving me thirty pieces, huh...? Ya know you could get this stuff for half the price if ya went to the city, right?" he asked, dubious at the deal that was too good to be true.

But the merchant just smiled gently. "It's perfectly fine. Just think of it as a tip or a token of my friendship. I hope we continue to do business in the future."

"If that's the case, I guess…," stated the chief sheepishly.

Truth be told, he was worried he'd displease the merchant by insisting it was too much, which might cause him to actually demand his money back. He fretfully stowed the coins away in his breast pocket without so much as another peep.

As Manju watched the chief squirrel away his gold, he chuckled to himself and called over the beauty of a maid, who was playing with the children a little ways off. "It's about time we get going."

"Understood," she replied.

"Aw, Miss, will you come visit again?"

"Oh, and please bring more candy next time!"

"As long as you're on your best behavior," she replied.

The village children were fond of her already and sad to see her go, especially when it meant they'd get no more candy, a rarity in their small community.

As Manju watched the kids shout goodbye, he continued to flash his genial smile, hopping into their horse-drawn cart, which was jam-packed with goods. They set out toward the northwest.

When the chief realized where they were heading, he called after them in a panic. "H-hold on a sec, you're not thinking of going to Dog Valley, are ya?!"

"Yeah, is there a problem?"

"Are ya outta your mind? Them evil demons are up that way!" he appealed to the brazen merchant.

Blood continued to drain from his pale face as he recounted this horrid tale.

"Listen up. About a month ago, some demons appeared in an abandoned, untamed area called Dog Valley. These were the same creatures that the Divine Goddess sealed in the bowels of the earth, the same foul beasts in the legends and the myths. Boar Kingdom sent six thousand of their soldiers to exterminate these unsavory vermin, but the army was wiped out almost immediately. Even the Goddess's heroes ran away in fear of their lives.

"I'm telling ya this for your own good. Ya got to take a different road," he concluded in a last-ditch effort to make them reconsider.

He was implying they'd get ripped to shreds with no guards to escort them through the occupied lands.

But his customer blew off his concerns and let out a loud guffaw. "Ha-ha-ha, there's no need for you to worry. We came through Dog Valley on the way here, and there wasn't a single *evil* demon."

"Y-you're lying!"

"It's the truth! The fact that I'm here is proof enough. There are no *bad* demons there."

"B-but...," he protested.

The village chief wasn't so sure just yet. After all, he'd seen the soldiers carrying back their fallen comrades with his own two eyes.

The merchant assumed that was the case. He didn't press the point any further.

"We'll come by and buy some more food from you sometime soon. When we do, just remember: It's *perfectly safe*," he stressed, though he didn't say specify what "it" was.

The chief was dumbfounded as he saw them off and watched them head toward the northwest.

When they were far enough away to no longer see the village in the distance, the merchant and his maid finally undid the *Illusion* spell.

"Oh man, those stereotypes about demons really run deep."

He had transformed from an average merchant to his original form: a black-haired boy. He wasn't bad looking, per se, but his crude personality was somehow clear on his face. But even as he said this, Shinichi Sotoyama didn't seem too bothered, although he let out a small sigh.

Next to him, the maid with blue hair also melted into her real appearance: a demon. She had dark skin, silver hair, and—last, but not least—long, pointed ears.

"I knew they felt this way, but it wasn't fun listening to them insult demons in front of me," remarked the Demon King's maid, Celes.

Her brow crinkled slightly in displeasure.

"I mean, even though they're the ones who started a war, we ended up killing half their army. And that's a fact," said Shinichi.

Well, to be exact, the fallen soldiers were resurrected using magic, meaning the death toll came to a grand total of zero. But the once-dead harbored some really intense fears and anger toward them, and he knew these feelings wouldn't go away that easily.

More importantly, the Goddess Elazonia spread the message far and wide that "all demons are evil." With her religious teachings in the hearts of many, it would be no easy task to overcome these stereotypes and prejudices against demonkind.

"That's why we're left with improving your image little by little," he continued.

They'd tour a bunch of villages to buy things at ten times the retail price. He would build his reputation as a generous merchant and keep drilling in "Dog Valley is safe" and "I've actually done some business with the demons without any problems." Over time, these rumors would spread and change the public's perception of them.

"The older generation is more hardheaded, so it'll be harder for them to turn their backs on the Goddess's teachings. To them, prejudice *is* common sense. But children take time to develop that awareness. Meaning they can see the demons for what they really are."

"Which is why you told me to give candy to the children," realized Celes.

You're a dirty, rotten scumbag. Her face contorted in disgust.

His eyes snapped open. In their day-to-day interactions, she always wore an expressionless mask, and this was a rare sight indeed.

"Are you angry that I'd take advantage of kids? Hold up, Celes, do you like children?"

"And if I said yes?"

"I'd say you have a surprisingly gentle side. I think you'd make a wonderful mom," teased Shinichi, mocking her with that annoying little smirk of his.

At each and every opportunity, he tried his very best to come up with the weirdest comment he could to get a rise out of her. He wanted to see her composed expression slip off her face in anger or embarrassment.

But she wouldn't keep taking punches.

Leaning closer to his face, she squeezed her large breasts together between her arms as she breathed into his ear, "I want to make lots of children."

"Agh!" Shinichi sputtered.

He hadn't expected such a critical hit. In his flustered state, he yanked on the reins of his horses, causing them to whinny in annoyance.

As he continued to cough and calm down, Celes turned away from him.

"Just as I thought," she remarked dispassionately. "You can't handle these kinds of jokes."

"You always take it too far!"

"You started it," she retorted aloofly. Her face was still cast down.

As he stared at her, something clicked in Shinichi's brain.

"Celes, did you make yourself blush?"

"I'm not blushing."

"Okay, sure, if your face isn't red, lemme see it."

"I'm not blushing," she stubbornly denied.

As he continued to seek revenge and press in on the dark-skinned elf, his lips quivered into another dirty smirk.

Their cart inched closer to Dog Valley, and the horses neighed as if to tell them, *Get a room, you two!*

Sandwiched between the slopes of two mountain ridges was a valley known for its hard and infertile soil. Little would be gained from

turning over its land, and the amount of labor required to develop it would be disproportionate to the profit. It made sense why all neighboring countries had abandoned it.

But even under these dire conditions, Dog Valley had a sprawling plot of land with soft, freshly tilled soil—a real field of crops (currently under construction).

"Hey, everyone's really getting into it," commented Shinichi as he stopped the cart.

In the field, the pig-headed orc and bull-headed minotaur wielded humongous hoes, swinging them down with all their strength. In the midst of these colossal demons, one lone figure was whacking the ground with a plow, faster than anyone else.

When he waved at the crew, she ran up to him with a smile.

"Shinichi, welcome back!"

In a straw hat and some sturdy overalls, she looked like the picture-perfect image of a farmer's daughter. This was the ex-hero Arian, nicknamed Red for her shock of red hair.

"Glad to be back! Looks like you've been working hard," praised Shinichi with a wry smile.

In the span of two days, as they went to the village and back, she had managed to plow through the valley as far and as wide as his eye could see.

"Tee-hee-hee, I got a little too excited, knowing my strength can be used for something other than fighting," Arian admitted.

For as long as she could remember, she'd whirled around her sword involuntarily to make a living—first as a monster hunter and then a hero. In her book, a job that didn't require her to hurt anyone was a job worth doing, and though it was hard to imagine, she was having a blast working in the field.

"I'd sometimes help out at villages when I was traveling around with my mom. But I couldn't go all out, so I..."

"I guess it'd be a terrifying sight to see a baby girl gouging furrows." He stroked her hair in thanks.

Once again, he'd seen a glimpse of the pain she'd gone through to hide that she was a half dragon for fear of being persecuted.

"No one will complain about that here. Go all out."

"I will!"

To be honest, the demons were all meatheads. They were only interested in strength. Be strong, and they wouldn't discriminate against humans or half dragons or whatever.

That's why Arian, who was nodding energetically, no longer hid the scales at the base of her neck with her scarf. Her red scales glittered and winked as they caught the sun. They were the physical proof of her half dragonhood.

As they continued to talk, the demons took notice and stopped working to gather around them.

"Shinichi! Celes! Welcome home, *oink*!"

"Is this human stuff that we can grow in the fields, *moo*?"

In their curiosity, the orc Sirloin and the minotaur Kalbi plucked up some potatoes from the cart to inspect them.

"Yeah, I got some potatoes 'cause they're easy to grow," Shinichi explained.

Shinichi loved the sciences, particularly chemistry, so much that he had a few molecular structures stored in his brain. Unfortunately, the extent of his knowledge on farming was bits and pieces he picked up from TV shows and manga.

Even if he could cast *Search* to retrieve some long-forgotten memories, he wouldn't be able to recall something he didn't already know, of course. Meaning he didn't know the specifics of cultivating wheat or rice. That was why he picked potatoes, since he'd planted some in elementary school.

"I was talking to the villagers, and it sounds like it's too late for sowing them but, eh, it'll probably be fine."

In this world, the farmers sowed crops in early spring and harvested them in summer, and again in the fall and winter: two full harvests, just like on Earth.

It was early summer, and the days were getting warmer. The crops would grow a bit more slowly since they were planted at the wrong time, but it was more important to gain experience sowing, tending, and harvesting.

Arian smiled in agreement through Shinichi's explanation.

"I've grown potatoes before," she beamed. "You're right! They're really easy to take care of!"

"Ooh, how do you do it, *moo*?"

"Umm, well, first you put them in the sun and wait for them to start sprouting, then you cut them in four—"

Kalbi paid full attention as Arian carefully explained the process in detail. Shinichi smiled in relief that they seemed to be getting along well.

Behind him, a small head poked out of the massive potato pile.

"Squee!"

"Oh, I forgot about this little guy."

The piglet was busy stuffing his face with potatoes. He was only about a foot long.

"Aw, how adorable!" Arian cried as she looked at the cute piggy with twinkling eyes.

"A-are you my brethren, *oink*?!" asked Sirloin, looking like he'd just reunited with a long-lost brother.

"There's no way we could do some large-scale animal-husbandry thing since we have, like, zero experience, but I thought we might try our hand at raising livestock with this one."

"Oh yeah, a pig is one of the easier animals to raise as livestock!" added Arian.

"…Uh, livestock?" blurted Sirloin. His pig face was frozen in place as he listened to their lively discussion. "You mean you're going to eat this baby, *oink*?"

"Once we fatten him up."

"You can't do that, *oink*!" cried Sirloin, wrapping his arms around the piglet and protecting him from Shinichi. "I wouldn't let you eat my sibling—even under an order from His Highness, *oink*!"

"*Squee!*" squealed the piglet as if to say, *Yeah, what he said.*

"Ah yeah, I had a feeling," claimed Shinichi with a dry smile.

He was unfazed by this reason. In fact, he expected it would happen.

It's kinda like how humans don't want to eat monkeys or chimpanzees. We see too much of ourselves in them. It'd be close to cannibalism. Shinichi was thinking something along these lines as he tried to come up with a way to persuade Sirloin.

However, Kalbi butted in to tell him off. "Sirloin, this is a sacred food, an offering to His Highness and Lady Rino, *moo.* You can't be so selfish, *moo!*" Kalbi slurped as he drooled and smacked his lips, staring at the piglet hungrily.

"Don't try to be all high and mighty! You just want to eat him yourself, *oink!*"

"Th-that's not true, *moo*! Besides, you've eaten boar before! Just eat pigs, too, *moo!*"

"Boars aren't the same as my brothers, *oink!*"

Celes observed the two squawking at each other and murmured to herself. "Maybe we should go buy a calf next."

"Don't go there," warned Shinichi.

It wasn't out of concern for the bull-headed minotaur—just that cattle required a lot more food than pigs, making them very difficult to raise.

"Anyway," he placated, "if you're that against it, we won't kill the pig."

"Really, *oink*?" The two pigs' eyes sparkled with hope.

"Yep, really." His smile was blinding. "We'll just take his meat without killing him."

"...*What?*"

"Well, if we fatten him up, we can shave off a little of his meat and heal him before he dies. Then we'll get meat forever, right? It's the perfect meat production system—made possible with magic!" revealed Shinichi, elated and impressed by his own awesome idea.

It could completely solve food shortages all around the world.

Everyone else, however, took a step back from him, their faces pale.

"Shinichi, that's so cruel…"

"I don't want to eat that. That's nasty, *moo*."

"If my brother is to go through that living hell, I would save him from his misery with my own hands, *oink*…"

"Are you perhaps the reincarnation of the Evil God?"

"What—?!" Shinichi cried in disbelief.

He shook his head, confused about how his totally amazing plan was rated so low. "Ugh, I guess I thought it'd be great, since this world doesn't have cultured meat or manufacturing plants yet …"

"It's not a matter of 'this world' or 'that world.' There's just something wrong with your brain," Celes shot back.

She was right: He'd face a ton of backlash against this plan on Earth, at least in the twenty-first century.

"Besides," she continued, "healing extensive wounds requires a lot of magic, meaning not many could do it."

"There is that problem, too."

It wouldn't be an issue if they were talking about a small cut or two. But it would require so much magical power to restore lost muscle—so much that only the Demon King, Celes, and Rino would be able to cast it.

They might need their energy to defend themselves. Sure, they'd made friends with Arian and defeated Bishop Hube, which meant the Boar Kingdom wouldn't be planning any attacks anytime soon, at the very least. But the Goddess's church could come after them at any moment. It'd be a real problem if they couldn't fight back because they'd wasted all their magic on food.

"Oh well, guess I'll cancel the 'Unlimited Pork Works' plan."

"Yay, *oink*!"

As Shinichi reluctantly surrendered, the two pigs let out a huge sigh of relief—along with Arian and the others watching over the scene.

"But if pigs and cows are out of the question, I guess we can raise… chickens?" started Shinichi.

"Lady Nugget the Harpy may object," quipped Celes.

"Okay, then let's raise horses."

"Sir Rumpsteak the Centaur may object."

"Okay, then we'll just eat slimes."

"Understood."

"Anything but that—!" cried Arian, rejecting Shinichi's off-the-wall suggestion with a bright-red face.

Truth be told, she was a bit traumatized about slimes, ever since she had been swallowed up by a super-powerful gluttony slime, dissolving her clothes and exposing her naked body to Shinichi. Even if that hadn't been the case, as a human, she was really hesitant to eat an evil monster.

"Hmm, but I bet slimes make great livestock, since I bet they'd eat whatever and multiply quickly."

"Shinichi, you're human, too, right? How could you be okay with this?" asked Arian.

"Er, well, it's pretty common to eat your defeated enemies in fantasy role-playing games."

It wasn't just that: He was Japanese. In Japan, they had no problem devouring crabs and squids—creatures once seen in the West as wicked monsters. They would even take extremely toxic puffer fish ovaries and pickle them. He carried the blood of his perverted foodie ancestors.

"Don't you wanna try some slime jelly made with giant frog oviducts?"

"Blergh…"

"How about jumbo pancakes made with roc eggs?"

"That sounds good!"

She might not have ever heard of the Japanese children's book *Gu——i and Gu——a*, but she was still the kind of girl who'd get excited if you mentioned giant pancakes.

"Right? And if you think about it, monsters are just animals, mutated 'cause they've been exposed to magic. Meaning they originally started off as your average cows and pigs, so it's totally fine to eat them," he reasoned.

"I—I guess?"

Her honest personality made her gullible. Not to mention, she was blinded by love. She took his words at face value.

As the dark-skinned maid watched this innocent girl being jerked around, she put a stop to it with a long sigh. "Would you please put your chitchat aside so we may go unload the goods into the castle's cellar?"

"Oh yeah. Arian, you want to come, too?" Shinichi asked.

"Yeah!" she replied, nodding happily and jumping up to sit next to him.

Seated between two beautiful women, Shinichi started the cart off toward the castle, a busty maid on one side and a flat-chested half-dragon hero on the other.

As the minotaur and other demons watched them depart and waved, they suddenly noticed the little piglet running around their feet.

"So what are you going to do with him, *moo*?"

"I will raise my brother as finely as I can, *oink*!"

"*Squee!*" the young piglet cried triumphantly.

He would later assume his position as the castle's pet and their food-waste disposal system.

The team split the heap of potatoes into two large piles. They carried the ones intended as seed potatoes to the cellar and the other half to the castle kitchen.

With the mountain of potatoes in front of them, they stood in the kitchen gripping their knives in tight fists.

"We will now begin the First Annual Potato Peeling Competition! Yeah!" belted Shinichi.

"I'll try my very best!" cried Arian.

"You're doing something strange again..." Celes observed the pair sharing an energetic high five. Nonetheless, she had a potato in hand, ready to go, despite her outward irritation. "But why go through the trouble of removing the skin? We could eat them as is."

"What? You'd eat it with the skin on?!" asked Arian incredulously. Her eyes snapped open in surprise at Celes's earnest inquiry.

It'd been a few days since Arian had come to live at the Demon King's castle. But she was still grappling with the stark difference in common sense between humans and demons, not to mention their base-level knowledge and customs.

"There are some ways to cook them with the skin on, like fries, but you generally peel them. Like, remember that soup we had at that tavern? It had peeled potatoes in it, didn't it?" he asked.

"Now that you mention it, yes," confirmed Celes, satisfied with his explanation. She brought her knife to the potato but stopped and tilted her head in confusion with a serious look on her face. "And how do I go about peeling one?"

"Yup. I had a feeling you were gonna say that." Shinichi nodded, charmed that the multitalented, steel-faced maid now reminded him of a cutesy, clumsy, clueless girl.

It wasn't that Celes was less skilled than others or a bumbling fool in the kitchen.

For starters, there was no way to save food in the demon world—not for want of trying—since demons were catastrophically disgusting. This meant there was no reason for demonkind to refine their cooking skills.

To a demon who'd only learned how to cut, boil, and roast things of random shapes and sizes, the task of peeling potatoes was an unimaginable, impossible assignment.

"All right, Chef Arian, please teach Celes the secret trick to peeling potatoes."

"Wait, me?!"

"I've pretty much only ever done it with a vegetable peeler. I figured you'd be better at peeling them with a knife."

"I guess I'm used to it, but I'm not sure if I'm good enough to teach someone," Arian blustered humbly.

She began to peel the potato in her hand.

Because she'd spent a long time traveling by herself and making her own food, she was a seasoned pro at removing their skins. It'd be going too far to say she was a trained culinary expert, but she neatly peeled its skin in ribbons in ten-ish seconds.

"Yep, that's how you do it," she announced.

"…My apologies. Could you from the top? What was the incantation again?" asked the maid.

"Um, no, well, I didn't use magic," Arian laughed wryly.

Celes still looked shocked, like a child who'd just been shown a magic trick. Arian wrapped her arms around the maid from behind, guiding her hands as they attempted to peel it together.

"Okay, don't move the knife. Rotate the potato instead—"

"Like this?"

The older of the two, Celes began nervously peeling the potato, a far cry from her deadpan, composed self, as the airheaded Arian guided and encouraged her. With this marvelous scene in front of him, Shinichi's face lit up with a smile.

"Ari-Cele, huh…? I totally support this!"

"What are you shouting about all of a sudden?" asked Arian.

"Pay him no mind. He always makes that face when he has something crude in mind," scoffed Celes.

Shinichi felt the ice from the maid's glare once she'd figured out his ulterior motive. He all but ignored her as he picked up a potato.

"Okay, the two of you peel a third of the potatoes and boil them. We'll bake and steam the rest of them."

Come summer, he wanted all the residents of the castle to taste the potatoes, to learn with their palates just how delicious their crop could be.

After delegating these tasks, Shinichi set a deep pot on the fire and poured in olive oil, the most expensive item from their little trip. Next, he took potatoes and cut them in strips, skins still on.

"What're you doing?" asked Arian, glancing in his direction, extremely interested in this new cooking method.

Shinichi grinned back at her as he dropped the stick-shaped potatoes in the oil.

"It must be hard work crushing and pressing olives. I mean, this oil was more expensive than I thought. I don't think there'll be enough for everyone to try it, but I wanted give our little princess a taste of the best potato dish ever."

He thought about all the chefs in the world, yelling at him for awarding junk food the title of "best dish," but he plated the fried potatoes and finished them up with some salt.

"I get the impression that french fries haven't been introduced to this world yet," Shinichi said.

An evil smile crawled across his face as he calculated how he could earn a killing from selling these. Shinichi took the plate for a taste-test to Rino, the seriously angelic daughter of the Demon King and the one who'd prompted the demons to set foot in the human world.

Facing the humongous door on the highest floor of the castle, Shinichi knocked on it politely. "Rino, are you there? It's Shinichi."

"Yes, I'll open the door," replied a voice from the other side, followed by the sound of small feet pattering toward him.

Slowly pushing the door open from the inside, Rino popped her head out, looking adorable with her lustrous black hair and ruby eyes.

"Shinichi, how can I— Wow, something smells really yummy!" Her eyes sparkled in delight.

"Mm, I was hoping you could eat this," proposed Shinichi, holding out the plate of fries to her.

"Wooow, what kind of dish is this?"

"We're going to grow some potatoes in the fields soon, so I took some of those and fried them in the oil from the fruit of the olive tree."

"Aw, I wish I could've seen you make them."

"Nope, the King would get angry if I let you in the kitchen."

Shinichi could see her helicopter parent lashing out in anger: *How dare you let my beloved daughter hold a knife! What if she cuts her tiny little hands?!* That was that, so unfortunately, he couldn't let Rino help with the cooking.

Anyway, he'd entered the room at her invitation. With the ceiling high enough to accommodate the ten-foot-tall Demon King, the room had a small canopy bed and a cute table—perfectly tailored to Rino, who was just under four feet tall. It looked like a mismatched miniature dollhouse.

"Here, eat up," he announced, setting his plate on the round table.

"Thank you," she beamed politely before stretching out her hand.

At first, she was a bit taken aback by their scorching hotness, but when she popped one into her small mouth, her eyes grew round in surprise. The oil and salt burst with flavor on her tongue, and she marveled at the texture of the potato.

"Wooow! The outside's crispy, but the inside is fluffy and light! And the surface is salty, but that mingles well with the subtly sweet potato inside! It's wonderful!"

"Rino, you have exactly what it takes to become a food critic."

Unlike the rest of demonkind, Rino had one of the few sophisticated palates capable of fully appreciating the flavor profile of french fries.

"It's so yummy, Shinichi. You must be a genius if you can make this!"

"I'm flattered, but a real chef could make these fries ten times more delicious, you know."

"T-ten times?! Human talent is not to be reckoned with..." Rino gulped. Her eyes were round again, but she didn't stop reaching for more fries.

"Once we've got a steady supply of ingredients—well, more importantly, once this fight with the humans is over, we can hire a real chef."

Maybe they'd summon a chef from Earth, just like how the Demon King had brought Shinichi to this world. That said, they needed to settle this feud with the Goddess's church first.

Shinichi glanced around the room and noticed a bunch of dolls scattered on the bed. "Rino, are these yours?"

"Yessiree. They're toys that one of the Grandpa Dwarves made for me."

"Toys, huh...?"

As Rino beamed happily at him and giggled, he turned away from her so she couldn't see the indescribably strange expression forming on his face. He inspected the dolls, all carved from wood, stone, and other materials. Their exquisite craftsmanship spoke to the skill of their creator. But—

"A dragon, a chimera, a Cerberus. They're more like monster action figures than dolls."

These toys all looked like they were meant for boys, a far cry from the cutesy, girly ones.

"Wouldn't you prefer some cute animals like rabbits or squirrels or something?"

"Rabbits? Squirrels?"

"...Sorry, I didn't realize they don't exist here."

As he looked at Rino shake her head in confusion, he was hit again by culture shock.

It made sense, after all: The demon world obviously had demons stomping around, making it an unforgiving environment for normal animals in the human world and on Earth.

"Better that than monstrous rabbit men or bunnies hop, bop, bashing your head in, I guess..."

That said, he was disappointed there weren't any natural-born bunny girls in the demon world. He looked forlornly at the dolls, finding one that was relatively girly—a mermaid—and picking it up.

"They really are well made," he remarked.

"Because the Grandpa Dwarves are really good at making things," praised Rino, finished with the last of the fries and delicately wiping her hands with a handkerchief. She came and sat down next to Shinichi. Picking up a doll, she said, as an introduction, "This three-headed doggy is Mr. Woof, and this cat lady is Ms. Meow."

"Yup, I'm relieved that your names are still cute and girly."

With a bull-headed minotaur named Kalbi and a pig-headed orc named Sirloin, he was worried she'd follow suit and name them in this cruel way.

"Have you named them all?" he asked.

"Yep, because they're my precious friends. We all play together when Daddy and Celes are busy," she reported with a smile.

"Oh yea— Huh? Hold on," interjected Shinichi, carried away by her peppy tone at first. "Rino, don't you play with your friends?"

The air in the room frosted over with a sharp crack. For the first time in his entire life, Shinichi thought he could hear it freeze over.

"……"

"Um, Rino?"

"Mr. Woof and Ms. Meow, they're my friends, right?"

"No, I didn't mean the dolls…"

"You and Arian and everyone else are my friends, right?"

"Yeah, I'm glad you consider me a friend…"

"Mr. Kalbi and Mr. Sirloin and Uncle Dwarf and everyone in the castle are my friends, right?"

"I'm sorry!" cried Shinichi, pressing his forehead to the ground as he groveled.

Rino continued on like a broken record, listing her friends with black, lightless eyes.

I guess she doesn't have any friends…

Now that she mentioned it, Shinichi couldn't recall a single child around Rino's age being in the castle. And it'd been quite some time since the King had summoned him.

He didn't know the reason behind this, but he nervously stood up to flee from this awkwardness. "W-well, I need to help make dinner, so I should get going…"

"Yep, I'll be playing with *everyone* here, so I won't be sad or lonely or anything."

"Okay, first, we'll play cat's cradle. It's a traditional Japanese game," started Shinichi, planting his butt on the ground again.

He lost his will to leave in face of her brave little smile and the tears forming in the corners of her eyes.

I've got to do something about this.

He found a string long enough to make a Jacob's ladder, and she clapped her hands in excitement.

Shinichi had just discovered his next mission.

After cat's cradle, they played a word chain game, then he showed her how to juggle, which made Shinichi feel a bit nostalgic.

A knock came at the door.

"Lady Rino, dinner is ready," called out Celes as she entered the room. She sighed when she saw Shinichi juggling four gold coins and glared at him. "I wondered where you'd gone to slack off. It seems you were showing off your gold to Lady Rino."

"Stop with your suggestive word choice!" Shinichi retorted loudly.

She always treated him like some sort of sex offender.

Celes ignored his response and gently pushed Rino out of the room. "We're going to taste the potatoes with everyone in the courtyard."

"A meal with everyone? That sounds like so much fun!" exclaimed

Rino, her eyes glittering in excitement. She was already hooked on french fries and potatoes, and she ran out of the room toward the courtyard.

After he sent off this childish, energetic figure with a genial smile, his mouth drooped into a frown. "Why doesn't Rino have any friends her age?"

"Well…it might be faster to ask His Highness," answered Celes, sighing heavily.

She'd expected that question and beckoned Shinichi to follow her. The two walked down flight after flight of stairs before arriving at a heavy iron door underground.

"What's the King doing in here?" he asked.

"You will understand once you take a look," replied Celes as she cast a *Clairvoyance* spell on Shinichi.

In the next moment, he saw through the iron door and stone walls, peering at the scene beyond them. Inside a domed room, he observed two people locked in a fierce battle. One of the contenders was a ten-foot-tall, blue-skinned giant. It was someone Shinichi was well acquainted with—the Blue Demon King Ludabite Krolow Semah.

And his competitor was the same exact Blue Demon King.

"What the—? Is that a doppelgänger?!"

"He's not one of us. He's a copy that His Highness created using his magic," Celes explained.

Even with this clarification, Shinichi couldn't tell between the perfect copy and the real King. After all, they were equal in ability: They both had enough strength to easily crush boulders into dust and enough magic to reduce the average human into ash.

"There wasn't anyone His Highness could train against with all his might, which was why he created a copy of himself to fight and further train his skills," she continued.

"Sure, I bet he's the world's best sparring partner, but…"

To be honest, he was a bit exasperated knowing that, like father like daughter, they were both loners. But he couldn't tear his eyes from the otherworldly fight between the King and his copy unfolding right in front of his eyes.

He stepped in close to throw a punch at point-blank range, casting an explosive attack spell and blasting off his arm. He used magic to heal and regrow it in the blink of an eye, countering with a round-house kick. But he seemed to expect the other King to dodge the attack, and he set a mine in the form of a *Thunder Ball*.

Both of them seemed to be reading their opponent's moves well in advance—sometimes attacking deftly from behind, sometimes crushing the other from the front, physically and magically pushed to the limit.

It was a demonic duel beyond human comprehension. This was the full extent of the Blue Demon King Ludabite's power.

"For your information, this isn't the full extent of his power. He's expending a significant amount of energy maintaining this copy and a *Protection* spell on the room, which means he can only use less than half of his true capacity," clarified Celes.

"Less than half…"

From the moment Shinichi had watched the King swat away the five heroes like flies, he knew the Demon King was unimaginably strong. But this was a whole new level of absurd. Sure, the undying heroes wouldn't die due to a technicality, but he really couldn't imagine how anyone would be able to take down the Demon King.

"By the way, Celes, can I ask you something?"

"What is it?"

"I'm under the *Clairvoyance* spell, but I still can't see through your clothes."

"A *Counter Magic* spell protects a girl's modesty."

"Dammit!" cried Shinichi, collapsing to the ground and pummeling the floor with his fists.

She'd just crushed one of his top three erotic fantasies: "An Unlimited, Clairvoyant View of Naked Girls!"

On a side note, "Slime Play" was another one, which Arian starred in brilliantly. There was still an ongoing debate (with himself, in his own mind) whether the last of the three fantasies should involve *Invisibility* or *Gender Changing* spells.

While the boy suffered in the throes of youth, the iron door loudly banged as it swung open from the inside.

"Hmph, Shinichi, Celes, why are you here?" asked the King.

"You must be tired from your training. I have come to call you: Dinner is ready," announced Celes as she bowed her head and cast healing magic on him to remove the remaining injuries.

"Oh, you're finished... You're not...the copy, are you?"

"You fool! You think I'd lose to a copy of myself?" The King snorted, laughing at Shinichi's rude question. "It is, in the end, just a copy. While we may be equal in strength, if I can predict its next move, the battle's as good as done."

"I see."

"It doesn't have a real desire to kill me. This isn't anything more than a warm-up." The King let out an unsatisfied huff.

To Shinichi, this stormy battle looked like hell on earth. To the King, however, it was his way of loosening up his tight muscles before the real fight.

"Just as I thought," he lamented. "I can only have a fulfilling fight with my wife." As he recalled his death matches with her, his face took on a look of nostalgia.

"Please stop," begged Celes, her face pale as she shook her head. "I would rather not see the two of you flatten down the mountain ranges again."

"Wait, what? Spine-chilling." Shinichi shuddered, blood draining from his face. Even atomic bombs wouldn't result in such a sight. "I mean, is your wife really that strong?"

"I guess I never told you. I fell in love with her strength the first time we fought, and I asked for her hand in marriage."

For so long, the King had been unable to find a suitable opponent, because his powers were overkill. But she was the first one who could stand toe-to-toe with him. They both felt fate drawing them together, knowing that they were each the only companion for them. Rino was born out of their love, crystalizing their romance.

"For the record, I was the victor by a thin margin. Because of that, my wife hasn't given up on a rematch. That's why she's been traveling the world, training to become a better fighter."

"Yeah, a match made in heaven," commented Shinichi.

He'd never met the King's wife before, but he'd never been so sure of something.

"Shinichi, did you come just to ask about our courtship?"

"No, I came to ask about Rino. Why doesn't she have any friends her age?" He finally broached his question.

The King's face contorted under his wrath. "Rino would become a bad child if she made friends!" he blared.

"...What are you talking about?" Shinichi wasn't sure what to make of the absurd reply.

Sure, he'd heard of tons and tons of parents pushing their children to make friends. But a parent who wanted the exact opposite? No way.

Celes looked at his dumfounded mug with a sympathetic expression but added to his unreasonable response. "We've tried to find playmates for Lady Rino, as His Highness and I are quite busy, but—"

"The daughter of a succubus tried to teach Rino how boys and girls do *@!^!" cursed the King.

"That definitely was the wrong choice," Shinichi said.

"When we fired her and hired someone else, the playmate turned out to be an incubus wearing girl's clothing! He'd hide and sniff her used socks!" he ranted.

"Is everyone in the demon world a pervert?"

As the Demon King ranted and raved, he got more and more cross with each successive story. No wonder he didn't want his daughter to make friends.

With great reassurance, Celes patted Shinichi on the shoulder. "Fear not. His Highness punished the incubus, who learned his lesson and changed his ways. We have no problems with him anymore; he's now a harmless man-lover."

"So your solution was to up his perversion by another notch?!"

"As long as he's harmless to Lady Rino."

"But he poses a threat to *me*!" shouted Shinichi, unconsciously covering up his butthole in case this incubus was still lurking around in the castle.

Celes returned to the topic. "That said, there are normal demon children as well. Not all of us are perverts. But few will volunteer to be Lady Rino's playmate. After all, she is the daughter of the Demon King..." She sighed heavily instead of continuing on.

"I can see how normal kids would be hesitant," Shinichi agreed.

If the playmate accidentally made her cry or hurt her in anyway, they would feel the King's wrath—if his anger stopped there. No, their entire family and distant relatives would also be reduced to no more than ash, even if Rino didn't mind what happened to her. With these risks in mind, the only people willing to volunteer had some sort of ulterior motive driving their actions.

"With the blood of His Highness and Her Majesty in her veins, Lady Rino is the best woman in the demon world, based on potential alone. Meaning lots of men want her to bear their children..."

"Which leads some morons to dress like girls to get closer to her. And you don't want to run the risk of accidentally exposing her to men. Got it," Shinichi concluded.

With all this in mind, they wanted to find a girl playmate, but there weren't many eager applicants so willing to risk their lives.

"Exactly. I trust you, but if you lay a single hand on my daughter... You know what will happen, right?" warned the King.

"You need not worry, Your Highness. I like big boobs, and I have absolutely no interest in little girls," declared Shinichi in a stiflingly formal tone.

He looked at the grinning King, who was patting his shoulder with enough force to hammer him into the ground.

"I understand your predicament, but don't you think bad friends are better than none at all?" he asked.

"Need I say it again? What would I do if Rino became a bad kid?!"

"That's what I'm saying. Being overprotective can't be good. If you tie her down too much, she'll end up with a twisted personality when she's older," Shinichi cautioned.

Next to him, a lightbulb went off in Celes's head. "I see, so you were subjected to bondage as a child."

"Do you really think I'm that twisted?" replied Shinichi.

As an aside: Shinichi's own upbringing had been pretty hands-off, so his argument didn't hold much water.

"Anyway, shouldn't you let her play or cook or do whatever she likes? If you control her too much, the stress will mess her up, you know. Someday, I bet she'll say something like 'I hate you, Daddy. Don't ever talk to me again—'"

"Gagh!"

"A critical hit?!"

Just by imagining this hypothetical situation, the Demon King started to cough up some blood as he took on the most brutal attack of the day.

"Geez, you love her too much..."

"Heh, you'd never find a father who loves his daughter more than I do, even if you searched this world top to bottom," replied the King.

"But just the other day, I swear I heard Lady Rino say, 'I love your candies the bestest in the whole wide world, Shinichi!'" added Celes.

"G-gack!"

"Celes?!" Shinichi shouted.

The King crumpled to the ground, convulsing in pain, unable to recover from her murderous attack. Even as she began to cast a healing spell on him, her stony expression didn't change one bit.

"In actuality, I'm not His Highness's maid, but his wife's attendant," she revealed to Shinichi.

"I see. I guess that explains why you treat him callously sometimes," he replied.

In her mind, the King's wife and Rino were both tied for first place, and the King was slightly under them.

"No matter what world they're in, dads always get the short end of the stick. Huh…" As he lent a hand to help up the crumpled King, Shinichi started to feel a little sorry for him. "Anyway, would you just think about the friend thing? You may be the Demon King, but you'll die someday, too, you know. You wouldn't want Rino to be alone, would you?"

"In other words, I should become unaging and immortal."

"What's wrong with you?"

Shinichi punched the King in his sculpted abdomen, but the only thing he hurt was his hand.

About a hundred demons of all different varieties and sizes gathered in the courtyard and smacked their lips as they tried the potato dishes.

"*Squeee!* All they did was bake it, and it turned out this delicious! This is a magical vegetable, *oink!*"

"The boiled ones are good, but the steamed ones are particularly soft and so wonderful, *moo!*"

"The ones that I think he said he…fried in oil? Yes, those french fries were so rich—exquisite."

"Hey! Share some with the rest of us! There aren't that many of those!"

The potatoes were baked, boiled, steamed, or fried. They were cooked using simple methods, seasoned only with salt. But to those used to eating torturously disgusting demon food, these potatoes were as delicious as a banquet in paradise.

"Hmm, these potatoes were produced outside the normal harvest season, so they're dried out and crumbly and not that great," Shinichi observed. His refined palate was used to the standards of modern Japanese cuisine.

"How greedy do you have to be?" asked Celes, sulking since she thought the food was perfectly delicious herself.

"Wooow, they're all so delicious! But I'm starting to feel full," Rino mused sadly, looking down at her bloated tummy.

In one hand, she held a baked potato. In another, a steamed potato.

"No need to overdo it. There's still tons of food left over," consoled Arian with a smile.

As he watched over his daughter, the Demon King grinned from ear to ear, before swallowing down a bowl of potato soup in one gulp. "Mm, nothing else matters as long as my Rino is happy."

"Then would you consider the friend thing?"

"Now, everyone! Today you may eat to your heart's content!" boomed the King, completely ignoring Shinichi's request as he held up a refill of the soup.

The demons cried together in joy.

That was when they noticed something.

"...Hmm, what could this be?"

"...Is it human?"

"...What is this incredible magical power?!"

The Demon King, Celes, and Arian all looked toward a mountain in the southwest.

"What is it?" Shinichi asked, curiously peering in the same direction.

Just then, a blinding white beam surged toward them, tearing through the burning red sky over the setting sun.

"What the?!" Shinichi was frozen in place, unable to move.

"HYAH!" The Demon King sprung from the ground, leaping high into the sky. From his outstretched palm sprung out an enormous wall of light, enveloping the entire castle. *"Fortress!"*

This seventy-foot white beam pierced the wall of blue light: one a destructive light to eradicate everything, one a protective light to save everything.

The two forces pressed back and forth, grinding against each other for three more seconds until the white light narrowed and disappeared, like water turned off from a faucet, and it was over.

"Was that like a laser beam attack from those robot movies...?" stuttered Shinichi, horrified by the sight of something straight out of a sci-fi film.

"I don't know what you mean by *beam*, but it was indeed a magical light attack," explained Celes.

"He's just so amazing...," marveled Arian, looking at the King in awe and great respect.

As the Demon King descended in front of them, the corners of his mouth twitched and pulled up in amusement as he examined the slight burn on his palm.

"Rejoice, Shinichi! Another hero has appeared," he belted.

"You're the only one rejoicing, Your Highness," Shinichi angrily pointed out.

But the demons witnessing this disquieting attack squealed in excited voices. Their cries of joy over the potato dishes paled in comparison.

"Whooaa?! There are humans other than Arian who can hurt His Highness? I guess humans aren't half bad, *oink*!"

"Is this hero a magic user, *moo*?"

"Let's all spend a little bit more time worrying about how we almost turned to ash. How does that sound?" Shinichi interjected in a calm tone.

But the meatheads were all so worked up and making such a racket, they didn't hear him. There was one other person who shared his undemon-like sentiment: Rino and her pure heart.

"Are Mr. and Mrs. Human attacking us again...?" she asked, frowning.

She'd thought the demons would be able to live in harmony with the humans now that they'd made friends with Arian.

Shinichi sighed gently as he stroked her head in an attempt to console her.

"Okay, so more heroes have arrived at the scene, huh? To think they can unleash a *Fire Attack* spell that reached us from that distance…

Their newest enemy pinned them using their firepower from a distance so far the demons couldn't promptly counterattack. It was a simple but highly effective tactic. It was particularly inconvenient for them, since their defense mechanism was the castle itself, which couldn't possibly be moved to a different location.

"They're hoping to blow away the castle and the King along with it. How is that *heroic* in any way?" Shinichi muttered.

This was a savage tactic, thought of at least once by every single video game player in the world. In the games, it was impossible to do. And yet, here they were on the receiving end—in real life.

Shinichi kept his grim expression as the King smiled brightly and heartily patted his back. "The enemy has fled using teleportation. I will leave the counterattack to you. I must stay here to protect the castle and my people."

"Yep, yep, understood, Your Highness," Shinichi said halfheartedly.

Despite his dispassionate response, he pulled out his smiley mask for the first time in a while, graciously accepting the command as the Demon King's advisor.

"So what is the hero like?" he asked.

"More accurately, *heroes*. There were about thirty of them."

The attack only lasted a moment, but sure enough, the King was able to see the number and identities of the enemy attempting to hide on the mountaintop.

"There were thirty heroes?!" blurted Shinichi.

"No, I'm guessing the person who cast the spell was the only hero. The rest were just extras, channeling their magic to the hero," replied the King.

"So they're like the spare batteries."

On a previous occasion, Shinichi had witnessed Bishop Hube borrow magic from other believers to cast his *Resurrection* spells. It seemed this was the same kind of case.

"Well, even if they had the others there for support, they must be a skilled magic user to wield that much magic at once," mused the King.

"I guess a normal person wouldn't be able to handle this amount of magic and not explode from the inside out."

"Shall we test it out?" Celes asked.

"No!" shouted Shinichi in a panic, avoiding her outstretched hand as she tried to put him under the same magical force. "Anyway, what was the hero like?"

"She was a girl about Arian's age, wearing all white with long blonde hair."

"Hmm, that description could match almost anyone," remarked Shinichi in grave disappointment.

Next to him, however, Arian's eyes snapped open in sudden realization. "Same age as me...maybe she's the Saint?"

"You know her?" he asked.

"Yeah, well, I've never met her in person," Arian clarified. "When I went to the Archbasilica of a certain Holy City for a job, a priest showed me around and said there was a prodigious magical hero about my age."

"The phrase *magical hero* sounds so redundant."

As someone intimately familiar with a certain famous role-playing game, Shinichi had been convinced that all heroes were masters in swords and magic.

"Her name was Sanctina, I think. I heard she's absolutely gorgeous and very faithful to the Goddess. Some people say she's the reincarnation of the Goddess herself," added Arian.

"Which is why she's the Saint. But if she's really her splitting image, she'd have...huge boobs." As Shinichi remembered the Goddess's ample bosom, his face split open into a wide, lewd smile.

"Hmph..." She huffed, crossing her arms over her own flat chest and puffing her cheeks.

The maid hit him with her coldest glare ever. "Defiling a saint and making her your own plaything? The epitome of dirty and twisted."

"That's not what I was thinking! Well, I mean, I *was* thinking that a saint was usually a character in the games like those female paladins, you know? If you let things get too far, they'd spit out, *Just kill me!* But I seriously wasn't considering going that far!" he frantically shouted, scrambling to put his sentences together.

"*Just kill me*?" Rino looked at him in confusion.

He really didn't want to find himself between a rock and a hard place, explaining to a little girl that a female paladin might tell her captors to kill her instead of letting them…

"Anyway." He changed the subject quickly. "I swear to defeat any and all of Your Highness's enemies—whether they're this Saint Sanctina person or not."

He covered his face with his grim mask.

This was how Shinichi's new battle to defeat the undying Saint began.

When the Demon King deflected the highest caliber of light magic, *Holy Torrent*, Saint Sanctina and her companions used their magic circle to flee from Dog Valley to the remains of the cathedral in Boar Kingdom. Despite their humiliating defeat, the Saint's well-favored face showed no sign of annoyance or impatience.

"Our Goddess is testing us. We will be one step closer to her paradise once we've destroyed that evil Demon King."

This paradise was only open to the devout followers of the Goddess Elazonia after death. In order to prove they were worthy of joining her, they were required to defeat the sinister demon creatures, even if it meant they died an honorable death—to be resurrected to challenge them once again.

Her determination to join the Goddess befit that of a devout follower, and the holy warriors all showered her with praise.

"You're absolutely correct, Lady Sanctina."

"Other than you, who else could possibly defeat the Demon King?"

"We will fight for you, our Saint, until our last drop of blood leaves our bodies."

As they faithfully took a knee in front of her, Sanctina smiled serenely over them. She was used to this kind of thing, even though they were far older than her.

"We might have failed this time," she began, "but we still have other means to defeat their wicked ruler."

That method was the strongest light magic known to man: *Solar Ruin*. It created a massive magic lens that stretched far in the sky to the distant horizon, gathering solar energy to scorch the earth's surface. It was the Goddess's divine punishment.

According to their teachings, she granted these powers to the first pope, who blasted away the heretical capital city Mouse using *Solar Ruin*. Many a painting depicted this divine moment: the magic lens sucking in the sun's rays, the midday sky transforming into an infinitely inky black, and the raging light and heat cascading onto the city like a waterfall—over ten thousand degrees Fahrenheit.

Sanctina's heart swelled in anticipation as she thought about how she, too, would be depicted in painting after painting at her moment of victory when she defeated the Demon King. She made no attempt to calm her beating heart.

"That said, we cannot defeat him as things are right now."

After all, even the first pope couldn't have cast *Solar Ruin* without the blessing and support of the Goddess. No matter how you looked at it, Sanctina and her measly thirty warriors couldn't muster enough power to wield such a magical abomination.

As she fell into thought with a troubled look on her face, one of her men spoke up. "Perhaps we should consult Cardinal Cronklum. He will grant us some of his wisdom and insight into our next move."

"Ah yes, a wonderful idea," gushed Sanctina, clapping her hands with a smile on her face.

Via telepathic message, she explained the entire situation to Cronklum in the Archbasilica.

"*Which is why I would like to ask for your assistance in destroying their fiendish king,*" she concluded.

"*I see,*" he replied without so much as a slap on the wrist for failing her mission. He suggested a solution: "*Head to the northern mining country, Tigris. They should have* you-know-what."

"*You-know-what?*" she asked, tilting her head in momentary confusion. But when Cronklum elaborated, she readily agreed. "*Yes, we would be able to defeat the evil Demon King using that.*"

"*Well then, I await good news.*"

With that, he cut off the telepathic connection and checked to see that no one was around. "That, and the people of Tigris don't have enough faith in our Goddess. What a great opportunity to remind them of the church's strength," Cronklum muttered to himself.

With defeating the Demon King and seizing the cynical country Tigris under his belt, he'd certainly be chosen as the next pope, no question about it.

"I'm counting on you, my beloved Saint."

As he thought of the day his expensive, faithful bloodhound would hunt a deer for him, his face broke out in a radiant smile.

At a tavern and inn in the Boar Kingdom, its middle-aged owner smiled in amused surprise when the black-haired boy and his maid paid him a visit.

"The boy's alive! When you didn't come back after your squabble with the Demon King, I thought maybe you'd gotten yourselves offed."

"Well, a bad penny always turns up, you know. Can't get rid of someone with a bad personality so easily," responded the black-haired boy.

"That ain't something to brag about," chided the owner as he handed them mugs of ale to celebrate their safe return.

As Shinichi took a seat at the bar, he gratefully accepted the beverage.

"Speaking of," the owner changed the topic, "I'm guessing little Miss Arian is okay, too?"

"Yeah, she couldn't come today, but she's doing well."

"Sir, I would like to order some ham and bread," Celes interrupted.

"Ah good, so the girl's all right," murmured the owner, looking relieved as he prepared her order. "I mean, I wasn't worried about her life, since she's one of them undying heroes, but with all those leaflets round town saying she was sexually harassed by the bishop and all, I was a bit worried she'd be feelin' down or something."

"Hmm? Is that what's been going on?" Shinichi had been the one to distribute those leaflets, but he feigned ignorance, ordering his own food and changing the topic instead. "By the way, is it true that this Saint lady or whoever is going to try her hand at defeating the Demon King next?"

Seeing that her attack spell blasted toward them from the southeast near the Boar Kingdom, Shinichi suspected she might have stopped here. His guess seemed to be on the mark, since the tavern owner nodded, looking a little impressed.

"You're quick on the uptake. I heard the church assumed ya failed and sent the Saint Sanctina to do the job."

"Could I please get the ham and bread to go? I would like to take it home," Celes interjected once again.

"Celes, can't you see we're having an important conversation right now? Take care of it later," warned Shinichi, implying that she needed to pay more attention.

"Nothing is more important than Lady Rino's food," she reminded him.

When dealing with all matters food-related, the maid became pretty useless, unable to respond or function properly. The owner smiled at the familiar sight of the two bickering, as he wrapped the ham and bread in a cloth.

He continued the conversation. "Speaking of Saint Sanctina, I've heard she's better at using magic than even the cardinals themselves. If ya get too sloppy, she'll beat the Demon King before ya know it."

"Well, since he already got us good, we were hoping to join forces with the Saint. Is she still here?"

"Bad timing," the owner grumbled. "I heard she was here until yesterday. Seems she's already gone somewhere else."

"Oh, huh. You don't know where she went, do you?" asked Shinichi.

The owner was stumped for a moment. "Hmmm, I definitely heard them saying she left through the north gate, so she'd probably be heading to the mining country, Tigris."

"The mining country?"

"Go north around Dog Valley to the foot of the Matteral Mountains. That's where their city is. The area's done really well from mining iron and gold, ya know."

"Hmm, I'd love to hit a gold-bearing vein and get rich quick."

"You and every other idiot out there. In fact, a bunch of them have already left to go and test their luck."

The government had already acquired the best mining areas in their territory, of course. The dream of striking gold would remain just a dream.

"There go my hopes of a gold rush... Anyway, why'd the Saint go there?"

"You think I'd know? Why don't you go ask her yourself," retorted the owner. He did give one helpful warning, though: "But I don't think you'll be able to be partners with the Saint."

"And why's that?"

"Rumor has it she's Cardinal Cronklum's favorite prodigy, so he's got her surrounded by a bunch of holy warriors to keep the less savory types away."

That's what one of his regulars said: that she had thirty men with her when she headed north.

"Unlike the wholesome little Miss Arian, this girl is a different story. I'd be willing to bet she'd never let a suspicious nonhero tag along," he continued.

"I wish I could just send in my application or something," joked Shinichi, hiding his frustration inside.

Well, I guess that'd be too *easy.*

In life-or-death situations, trust was more crucial than skill to unify a group. With her well-acquainted group of men and magical skills, she certainly had no reason to bring someone shady into her party.

More importantly, if she'd heard that Bishop Hube had accused

Shinichi and Celes of conspiring with the Demon King, it'd be dangerous to even show their faces.

"Oh yeah, what happened to Bishop Hube anyway?" he asked.

"Hm? He was called back to the Archbasilica. I think they were dealing with that leaflet incident and seeing if he was responsible for the cathedral collapsing. I heard a rumor they stripped him of his bishop title as punishment."

"Aw, that's too bad (*Heh-heh-heh, serves him right*)."

"*No need to telepathize your true feelings to me*," Celes quipped, gulping down the last of her ale. She was sick and tired of seeing him excel at keeping a straight face as he sneered dirtily to himself.

Shinichi took her finished drink as a signal, leaving some coins on the counter as he stood. "Thanks for the food. We'll come again."

"Yeah, and next time bring the little miss with you. Tell her no one believes those terrible rumors anyway," called the owner.

He already had his hand on the door, ready to leave, but he was so touched by the owner's concern for Arian that he paused and looked back.

"Hey, have you ever heard of french fries?" he asked.

"What's that?"

"It's a way to cook potatoes. Takes a lot of oil, so it's expensive to make, but I bet they'd go really well with ale…"

Later, these french fries—Shinichi's recipe–would become the talk of the town. Such a big hit, in fact, that the owner cried with joy at his new prosperity.

Shinichi and Celes went back to the Demon King's castle to drop off the food for Rino and pick up Arian before they headed to Tigris, the mining country.

"Have you been before, Arian?" he asked.

"Yeah, I used to stop by when I was a monster hunter. You can get iron pots and tools and things for really cheap there. Oh, and the quality's really good, too. You know, my old sword was made in Tigris!" Arian blabbed.

"Your old sword? More like a crude club."

"Well, I didn't have much money back then…"

At the time, she'd ordered a sword strong and thick enough that it wouldn't bend under her strength as a half dragon. With that, there just wasn't enough money left to put into sharpening or decorating the sword. She recalled this memory with nostalgia as she rubbed the dwarven-made magic sword now strapped to her hip.

"I don't think they sell magic swords, but their goods are so cheap and high quality that they even sell them in Boar Kingdom," she explained.

"So they profit from buying low in Tigris and selling high in Boar Kingdom," Shinichi excitedly theorized, catching his balled fist in his other palm.

This was a great bit of information. He turned to the maid. "Celes, I have a business proposition for you."

"I refuse to teleport."

"Tsk, you already figured it out, huh?"

Think about it: It took ten days to make a trip between Boar Kingdom and Tigris. With teleportation, they could cut down on travel expenses and the risk of highway thievery. Meaning they could sell at a lower price than the other merchants, monopolize the market, and make huge profits.

"Allow me to explain. The larger the object, the more magical power is required to use teleportation. Distance is also a factor, meaning I would be able to teleport, say, a cartload's worth of goods, only six times per day."

"Yeah, that's more than enough, you know."

Any average human magic user would be shocked at her nonchalance, turning pale as they wondered aloud what the hell this person was.

But Shinichi knew it would be a waste to make her use her magic on such endeavors, because she needed to cast spells to attack and find their enemies and disguise herself and Shinichi.

On top of that, he had no desire to make enemies of the merchants they drove into bankruptcy. Which meant this teleportation express delivery service would not come to fruition after all.

"That said, we'll eventually need to make money somehow," Shinichi muttered.

Sure, there were mountains of gold in the Demon King's castle. It wasn't like they were short on funds or anything. But he needed to remember it wasn't infinite. Because they were still in the early farming stages and a long way from self-sufficiency, they needed to spend a significant amount purchasing food from neighboring villages. Meaning there was a lot of output and no input, and he needed to secure some income to provide for their futures.

"If we had some demon-made exclusive specialty goods or something, I'm sure we'd be swarming with merchants eager to get a slice of their pie."

If they could barter and sell their souls for cold-hard cash, merchants would be the first people in line to sell, sell, sell. If the goods were tempting enough, he figured, some of the merchants would definitely find a way around the Goddess's teachings and start trade with the demons.

"And from there, we can establish trade with the humans, which will eventually lessen the prejudice against demonkind…" he babbled.

"Wow, Shinichi, you think about so many different things," marveled Arian, staring at his serious face in admiration.

"That's an advisor's job," replied Celes without much embellishment, but even she handed him some bread for lunch in gratitude.

They passed the time until they eventually arrived at Tigris.

Against the splendid backdrop of the Matteral Mountains stretching into the distance in both directions, they stood in front of the city walls. They were made from stone from the mountain range, stacked tall and thick before the city. It was formidable, more appropriate for an impenetrable fortress than a mining city.

"Well, I bet the Demon King could probably take it out in one hit," Shinichi bragged.

"He's kind of an exception to the rule, isn't he?" Arian butted in, smiling dryly.

To think these castle walls were nothing more than a piece of paper to the Demon King, and in comparison, how the heroes, much less the humans, would struggle and falter in front of this stony fortress.

There were floods of people and wagons coming and going through the city gates: miners going to work, people moving ore into the city, merchants stocking up on metal goods. The three slipped between the crowds and weren't stopped by the gate guards as they entered the city without a hitch.

"I dunno if it's because of their main industry, but there are a bunch of rough-looking guys around," Shinichi observed.

"I guess it makes sense. You have to be really strong to work as a blacksmith and stuff, too."

All the men walking down the road appeared strong, but there weren't many who were built like those macho weightlifters. They were mostly slimmer, like marathon runners.

I don't get the impression that this is how they want to look—more like they don't eat enough to build muscle.

As an aside, the use of magic in this world was limited to a select few, even though it was a power that far surpassed science. These favored few became court mages or priests, monster hunters or even heroes—they wouldn't end up tilling fields on some farm.

Due to magic and its convenience, there weren't many scientific advancements in this world—no combines, tractors, or other machinery, and certainly no pesticides or chemical fertilizer. This all meant their harvests were relatively small, and they couldn't get the food needed to put on weight like the modern Japanese.

But they don't seem to be starving, so that's good.

At the very least, they had potatoes, which were the closest thing to cheating the nutrition game. So maybe this world was well off after all.

Shinichi was lost in thought until he suddenly noticed the delicious smell of food wafting toward him. When he looked up, he saw a boy selling meat skewers from his cart.

"What's this?" Celes asked.

"Goat meat skewers!" Arian explained. "For a little extra, he'll melt some goat cheese on it for you!"

She flew to the stand in a flash. "I'll take every one you have," she ordered.

"Celes!" Shinichi scolded as he chased after her. "Stay!"

"Margh blamag glomarm." She chewed and swallowed. (Translation: Trying to train people like dogs? You're one dirty, perverted owner.)

Even with her cheeks bulging with grilled meat, she still didn't forget to take her usual jab at him.

"Eat or talk. Don't do both." Shinichi took a handkerchief out of his pocket and attempted to wipe away the cheese from her face. "Jeez. The first time I saw you, I thought you were a cool girl. Oh, why'd you have to turn out like this…?"

"If I hadn't known of such irresistible desires, I wouldn't have. You're the one who taught this innocent body to crave such naughty things."

"Could ya please stop with these innuendos?" Shinichi begged.

He couldn't deny he was the reason behind her heat for meat (totally nonsexual), but he never anticipated she'd turn into some cutesy, clumsy little girl. He couldn't take responsibility for that.

As he thought and let out a labored sigh, someone poked him in the shoulder.

"What's up, Arian?"

"Well, I thought the skewers were really yummy," she said, suggestively showing him the cheese smeared on her cheek as she chomped down her skewer.

"…You have something over here." Shinichi laughed dryly as he wiped her cheek with his handkerchief.

Her smile was full of pure joy. "Hee-hee-hee, thanks!"

"No problem," Shinichi replied bashfully, reaching for his own skewer in an attempt to hide his embarrassment.

As the boy at the skewer stall took the coins from Shinichi, he looked like he was ready to cry blood, gesturing wildly to the area around them. "Mister, could you go now?"

When Shinichi finally looked around, he realized a crowd of men had stopped on their heels, entranced by Celes and Arian. Oh, and they were seething with jealousy and envy.

"...I'm very sorry," said Shinichi, bowing his head deeply.

He took both their hands and fled, leaving behind the murderous rage of every bachelor there.

"Whew. You know you're both pretty, right? Could ya at least *try* not to do anything to attract any extra attention?"

"Aw, you think I'm pretty, tee-hee-hee."

"Flatter me all you want, but I will not hand over my meaty majesties."

"...Maybe I should've come alone," Shinichi moaned regretfully as he looked at Arian's blushing face and Celes chowing down.

But alas. That would be asking for too much.

As he continued to think, they started to head down a wide road toward the castle.

"Are we going to the castle?" Arian asked.

"No, I figured it'd be near the castle— Ah, yeah, there it is."

There, two hundred yards from the castle gates, was the building he had in mind. It was a bit smaller than the one in Boar Kingdom, but its blinding white walls gleamed and glittered in holy pride as it basked in the sunlight.

It was the Tigris Cathedral of the Goddess Elazonia.

"If the Saint is in Tigris, this is where she'd be."

"All right, let's check it out!" Arian shouted.

"No, wait a second," Shinichi called out, grabbing her as she turned to head straight into the cathedral. "People are gonna recognize you. They might recognize me, too."

"Oh yeah…" Arian's face clouded over as she thought this through.

This was because they could be captured the moment they stepped inside the cathedral, if Bishop Hube had spread the news of a certain black-haired boy influencing a redheaded hero to betray the church. With Celes by their side, they probably wouldn't lose if it came down to a fight. But their opponent was an undying hero, after all. They probably wouldn't win, either.

It'd be best to hide their appearances until they gathered enough information to form a plan that'd break her psychologically.

Well, in truth, he didn't need to exercise such caution. Sure, Bishop Hube testified something close to the truth, but he'd glossed over some parts to make himself look better: no mention of his love for Arian, his abusive behaviors, or how he was outwitted by Shinichi.

It made his whole story reek of lies.

From the perspective of the cardinals, who wanted to eliminate this imminent threat of a bishop, it served them best to explain his action as the divine retribution of their Goddess for his sexual misconduct against a young girl. This was the message that they spread to the rest of the church. In the end, they favored lies over truths and determined truths as lies.

Of course, there was no way for Shinichi to know this, so he was piling on one precaution after another.

"We could change our appearances with Celes's *Illusion* magic, but the magic users would notice, wouldn't they?"

"Yeah, it's pretty hard to hide the flow of magic power," Arian offered.

It was possible to fool someone if one magic user had way more magical powers than the other, but Arian was able to see though it, and before that, even Bishop Hube had noticed their efforts. Which meant they should assume the Saint would also be able to perceive the change.

"Do you think the clergy will throw a *Dispel* spell at your average devotee the moment they step into the cathedral?"

"Um, I wonder?" Arian's face twisted up. "It'd be incredibly rude to just go around dispelling *Illusion* spells that others have in place..."

"Why is that?" asked Celes aloud, having some difficulty understanding the finer details of human culture.

Shinichi answered in Arian's place. "Hey, you remember how you changed the appearance of the merchant with the burned face, right? It's the same thing. Sometimes people just have things they'd rather hide. It'd be rude to make that public for all to see."

"I see. That's right."

"Good. Even if Arian pads her chest, you just leave it alone, you got it?"

"Understood."

"I haven't done anything like that!" cried Arian, covering her flat chest, tears in her eyes at the unfounded accusation.

"That's why it's rude to randomly dispel the *Illusion*, but I doubt the members of the church would hesitate..." Shinichi trailed off.

"You two aside, it would be bad if they exposed my true form," Celes added.

One look at her long ears, and they'd know instantly that she was a demon, throwing them immediately into a hostile situation.

"Which is why we can't use magic. We need to find another way to change our appearance, like a hat or hair dye or—"

As they continued to discuss potential disguises, he glanced over and saw a man coming out what looked like a back door of the cathedral. Something about him made Shinichi feel very uncomfortable.

"Doesn't that guy seem, like, particularly weak?"

Sure, he had the burly build of a miner, but his legs were shaking so hard he looked like he barely had the strength to keep walking.

"Huh? Wait!" Shinichi exclaimed in a sudden burst of inspiration.

"You're wrong," replied Celes.

"I haven't said anything yet."

"Let me guess: You're thinking, *The holy Saint is letting young men play with her holey body at night?!* Right?"

"......" Shinichi didn't respond, averting his eyes.

"Your dirty, sex-obsessed mutt mind has gotten you in trouble again."

"……"

Arian suspected that Celes's mind was just as dirty for reading his thoughts, but she didn't say anything.

"I wonder what's tiring them out so much," he said.

Following the haggard man, the door opened again to let through an elderly woman and a child. All their breathing was ragged and their steps pained.

"I want to know what's going on inside, but we don't have time to look for a disguise…"

"There seems to be no *Counter Magic* on the building. I could look and listen in using *Clairvoyance* and *Wire Tap*, then share it with the two of you using a *Link* spell," Celes offered.

In the shadows of a nearby building, she joined hands with the two of them and chanted the incantation, evoking the images and sounds inside the cathedral. As she saw this in her mind's eye, she passed it on to the two humans.

"The architecture inside isn't all that different from the Boar Kingdom Cathedral, either… Ah, there."

At the very end of the cathedral was a prayer room, opulent and housing a statue of the Goddess and, in the center of it all, a single girl, surrounded by her holy warriors.

She had fair skin, platinum-blonde hair, and pure-white robes.

With a delicate flush of color on her face, she was reminiscent of a snow fairy, threatening to disappear at any moment. In contrast, her body was feminine and soft, formidable and taut in all the right places. She had an allure and sensuality that didn't quite match her age. This was the newest enemy of the Demon King: Saint Sanctina.

"I knew it! Nice rack!" Shinichi hooted.

"Good for you."

"Wait, she's the same age as me…?!" cried Arian.

All three of them had different reactions to her generous twin peaks, until their attention shifted to an item beside her.

"What the hell is that?"

It was a ten-foot-tall crystal, translucent and towering over them.

It hadn't been cut: Its surface was rough, left as it had been when pulled from the earth. But it was so bewitching that it sucked in the attention of those around it—the most beautiful gem of all.

"You guys don't remember seeing anything like that in the Boar Kingdom, right?"

"No, not even in the cathedral," Arian replied.

That meant this thing couldn't be some sort of tool for a ritual of the Goddess's church. They both cocked their heads in unison.

Next to them, Celes offered a possible explanation with uncertainty: "Could it perhaps be a magic conductor?"

"You know what it is?"

"Yes. But this is the largest one I've ever seen," she murmured. "That's why I can't be certain—"

But before Celes could finish qualifying her explanation, the Saint made a move.

"Next. Please come in," she called out.

"Y-yes."

A young man with a deep cut on his arm entered the prayer room. He was first taken aback by the huge crystal, then by her beauty, completely forgetting about the throbbing pain in his arm as his face turned beet-red.

The Saint didn't seem to notice, as she just smiled gently and held her hand over his right arm. *"Healing."*

A burst of light surged from her hand, healing his arm the moment it touched him.

"Thank you very much. This is my offering."

He held out a number of silver coins, hoping to touch her hand as he handed them over. But one of her burly warriors stepped in to take the money.

Crestfallen, he turned to leave, halting in his tracks when she called out to him.

"Please wait. Before you leave, could you offer your devotion to the Tears of Matteral?"

"I'm sure you're aware of the hellish bunch in Dog Valley. This is a ritual necessary to defeat them," one of the holy warriors expanded.

"Uh-huh...?"

He still didn't seem to understand at all, but a holy warrior prodded his back until he was standing square in front of the giant crystal. They started to pressure him to hurry up, get it going, placing his palm on the crystal.

As soon as he made contact, a blurry dim light poured out of his hand—and was quickly sucked into the crystal.

"Ah?!" he shrieked in surprise. He'd never experienced such biting coldness or overwhelming fatigue in his entire life, and his butt slammed against the ground as he fell to the floor.

The Saint continued to smile at him serenely. "I am very grateful for your cooperation. With your devotion and faith, we will definitely defeat the demonic clan."

"Your body will feel better after a good night's rest," advised another one of her men. "Please come again to offer your devotion to the Goddess."

"Not just you," added another. "Tell all your friends and family to come and offer themselves to her."

Their glares said everything left unsaid: *If you ignore our request, you'll never be healed in this cathedral again.* They yanked him by his shoulders, forcing him to stand and giving him a hard push out the back door.

As the Saint observed this scene, her plastic smile didn't waver or budge at all.

She called in another unsuspecting patient from outside. "Next," she said. "Please come in."

It went like that for a while. Men and women, young and old. All were robbed of their strength, kicked out into the streets as soon as the Saint was done with them.

Arian trembled with fury. "Why? Why would they do such a terrible thing...?!"

"To defeat the Demon King, of course," replied Shinichi, releasing Celes's hand, satisfied with what they'd seen. "I'm guessing that thing steals magic power?"

"Yes, these magic conductors are strange stones that can store magic power." Celes nodded as she explained.

She took one last look at the magic conductor—the Tears of Matteral—and undid the *Clairvoyance* spell. "They can collect magic to use for spells or make them into magical items. Well, take that with a grain of salt; I don't know all the details, and I imagine it'd be much faster to ask the experts, the dwarves."

"All right, I'll ask when we get back to the castle." He nodded back.

But as he watched another weakened mother and child punted out of the cathedral, his face contorted in disgust. "So they're thinking of gathering people's magic and casting a huge attack spell... You can't be telling me it's like a Spir—— Bomb."

There was no right way for the heroes of justice to defeat their enemies. But to dangle faith over these people's heads and coerce them to surrender... Well, this diabolical scene was just about enough to make him want to vomit.

"Just how many normal people would they need to gather in order to defeat the Demon King?"

"...I cannot say. But I can't say it's impossible," Celes replied, shaking her head back and forth.

If the Saint and her thirty men could collect their powers and slightly burn the King, imagine what they could do with the magic of tens of thousands of people. It might be strong enough to bear its blade at the Blue Demon King.

"Shall I destroy the magic conductor?" Celes was ready to totally eliminate this threat against her master.

"No, that's our last resort," he rejected, holding his hand up to reign in her in. "We have no proof that it's their only magic conductor. And if we destroy it, it'll just incite more violence and spur them to attack us with greater force."

Some agents of the demons destroyed the Tears of Matteral. They've infiltrated the city—an enemy to be feared! But this is proof that they're afraid of humans. Now lend your power to the Goddess again, and we shall banish this wickedness for good!

That's how they'd push the people to take action, and the situation would get worse for sure.

"Even if we assume that's their only magic conductor, they can achieve the same thing by leading everyone to the Demon King's castle," continued Shinichi.

Say they all came to the castle, combining the magic power of tens of thousands of people. The Saint could cast a powerful spell to vanquish the Demon King once and for all.

To be honest, that would be a really theatrical and cliché ending. Shinichi laughed wryly, knowing there was no way that day would ever come.

"And what if they're not your average Joes? If they bought together a few thousand heroes, they'd probably get the same effect."

"Why haven't they done that?" Celes asked.

Instead of answering right away, Shinichi asked Arian a question. "How many heroes are there all together?"

"Sorry. I only know of me, Ruzal, and his party," she replied sheepishly.

"…Oh sorry, I forgot you didn't have any friends." His face was serious.

"That's got nothing to do with this!" stammered Arian with tears in her eyes as he poked around at old wounds.

"Hey, don't worry about it. Rino doesn't have any friends, either—"

"Lady Rino may not have friends her age," Celes interrupted, "but she is loved by the residents of the castle as well as tens of thousands of her subjects in the demon world."

"Give it a rest. I don't think Arian can take any more! Her MP is dangerously close to zero!"

"…It's fine. I've got you, Shinichi."

Celes really didn't mean anything by her attack, but Arian stuck her nose in the air, hugging her knees to her chest. Shinichi tried to comfort her for a while before returning to the topic at hand.

"I'm sure there's a bunch of reasons why the heroes don't come together to do a combined attack on them: Maybe there aren't enough heroes or they're shorthanded as they fend off other monsters or their schedules don't line up."

On top of that, there was the political war between the cardinals for the papal appointment. But Shinichi wasn't familiar with the ins and outs of the church's internal affairs. There was no way for him to guess this was the case.

"To put it simply, they don't view the Demon King as so imminent a threat that they'd need to throw all their collective power into attacking him," he guessed.

"So they underestimate us?" Celes's forehead wrinkled in annoyance.

But they needed to be thankful. That was the only reason the demons hadn't been annihilated yet.

"It's over for us if they wage an all-out war and gamble with the lives of humankind. I hate to say it, but I have a feeling that the Demon King could still win against them… Anyway, if it came down to that, Rino would propose to retreat back to the demon world."

"Right."

At the very least, this battle wasn't a fight to the death with only one victor. Right now, their only goal was to create an environment for the peace-loving Rino to eat as much as she liked.

As for Shinichi's ulterior motive, well, that was to create a country where everyone could live happily, regardless of birth or race or if they were human, demon, or half dragon.

"Destroying the magic conductor is our last resort, since it'll lead to war for sure. And anyway…" Shinichi held his breath for a moment, stopping to allow his most evil smile to ooze across his face. "Wouldn't it be more interesting to steal that magic conductor and use it for our evil deeds?"

"You're sick," Celes spat, as Shinichi's imagination ran away with him, gleefully thinking about turning it into a magic storage bank and making magic robots. "What is our next move if not to destroy the magic conductor?"

"Hmm, yeah, that..." He lapsed into thought for a moment. "You see, the magic conductor could be replaced even if we took it. We gotta take out the Saint. That's irreplaceable."

"Are you going to flirt your way into a young maiden's heart again?" she commented in her vexed tone.

"Huh?!" interjected Arian, shooting up from the ground, forgetting her stubborn act. Her face changed suddenly to reveal a brokenhearted expression, as she clung to his chest. "You're gonna do the same thing to that Saint as you did to me?"

"No, that—"

"Are you going to be nice to her, too? Make her pancakes? See her naked? Lick her neck?"

"Calm down, Arian. You're blurting out some pretty crazy things!"

"Ah..." Arian clamped her hand over her mouth and looked at Celes.

But the maid didn't seem surprised at all. "If you're referring to what happened in the inn, I saw everything with *Clairvoyance*. There's no need to hide anything," she assured.

"Why would you tell her?!" belted Shinichi, but he was too slow to stop her.

"Y-you saw...everything, all that...?" Arian stuttered.

Her face turned white in fear, then red in shame, as she realized what this all meant.

"NOOOOooooo—!" she wailed in despair as she dashed off toward the horizon, a step toward tomorrow.

But, of course, considerate as she was, she deployed her jumping skills to bound over the rooftops, careful not to injure people on the streets as she sprinted away.

"You don't have to run away like that...," he called after her.

"As friends, I thought we shouldn't have any secrets between us. This isn't what I intended ..." Celes shifted awkwardly.

"Wait, this is you being *considerate*?" asked Shinichi, fed up with this entire situation.

"At any rate, what shall we do next?" she asked, getting back on topic after they slipped out of the growing crowd, gathering to watch the scene.

The two walked farther into the buildings' shadows.

"Let's put all this talk about seducing her aside. The best thing would be to build a friendship with her and get her to understand the demons' situation, but..."

"Wouldn't that be difficult?"

"Yeah..." He sighed, at a complete loss. "As the old man at the tavern said, there's a bunch of those holy warriors at her side. There's just no way to get close to her."

Well, he could probably suss out a time when she was alone by monitoring her schedule and daily routine. He'd be able to make contact with her more easily if they were alone. But even if he could, the holy warriors would interrupt and berate him, meaning it would take a long time to build a strong relationship.

"If we dawdle and loiter around, they'll fully charge the magic conductor."

"Meeting with Arian for the first time was much easier than this," Celes recalled.

They didn't have a time limit, she was a loner, and she was straightforward to the point of gullibility.

"Compared with that... No, we can't give up before we even try," Shinichi interrupted himself, shaking off a bad feeling and lifting his face to look forward. "Either way, I want to find a way to get close and make contact with her! For that reason—"

"Yes?"

"Let's find Arian."

"...My sincerest apologies."

With Celes and her unusually sincere apology, Shinichi headed off toward the horizon, toward tomorrow, where their wholesome girl had disappeared.

The castle of the Tigris Kingdom was unadorned, as the builders had its practicality in mind. But the rough-hewn walls and floors were decorated lavishly with valuable paintings and rugs, symbols of the country's wealth as a major exporter of metals.

Saint Sanctina sat in its waiting room, ignoring the tea and cakes in front of her, staring down the minister across from her.

"Are you telling me that I cannot meet with His Highness again?"

"My deepest apologies. His Highness has suffered from an illness since boyhood, and his condition is not well enough to meet…"

Sanctina sighed through her smile as the minister babbled on and on. He was clearly well into his sixties, but his hair was oddly thick for his age.

"You put me in such a predicament," she said. "I'd hoped to ask His Highness to issue a decree to his people…"

…to gather their magic power into the giant magic conductor, the Tears of Matteral, and obliterate the unholy ruler of demons.

They had set off on this plan as instructed by Cardinal Cronklum, but they hadn't made as much progress as they thought they would. They took the magic powers of the injured and the few true devotees, but as rumor spread across town, none of the citizens dared come closer to the cathedral. Even though the townspeople couldn't use magic, this process left them feeling so exhausted that they couldn't work at all for a full day. Given this, it was unsurprising that they wouldn't go near the cathedral.

But Sanctina couldn't sympathize with these commoners. After all, she'd been isolated her entire life, kept at the cardinal's side ever since she was born. Never once in her sheltered life had she experienced hunger or cold.

Without her knowing, the holy warriors were secretly coercing the people to give themselves up to her, scraping together a few hundred people per day. But it still wasn't enough.

That's why they'd wanted to have the Tigris king issue a decree to the people, calling for their cooperation, but they had so far faced rejection after rejection on the basis of his health.

"Minister, could you not issue the decree in his place?"

"The Kingdom of Tigris is under his rule. Even though His Highness had been sick as a child, a retainer issuing a decree is an act that can never be forgiven."

"Well then, when would we be able to meet with His Highness?"

"We are doing everything we can, but I am uncertain as to when..."

The minister took his time to answer her inquiries politely. But as a true politician, he evaded setting a meeting time in stone.

If their entire population collapsed from lack of magic power, their economy would grind to a complete halt for two—even three—days. Not only would their coffers take a serious hit, the people would also be bursting with raging discontent. This meant they had absolutely no desire to make a decree to force all the citizens to pour their magic power into the Tears of Matteral.

As the minister ducked and evaded her requests, one of her men behind her erupted in anger in her place. "This again?! You're mocking us with these obvious bald-faced lies about some bogus illness!"

Their previous king had died two years earlier from an illness, meaning the current ruler inherited the throne quite young. If he were actually sick, their entire kingdom would be on edge. But his reign had been calm from the very beginning, and there wasn't any indication of unrest among the people.

In other words, this disease was imagined as a way to deny their request to meet with the king.

Even though the holy warrior saw through his deception, the

minister didn't let his true thoughts show at all, shaking his head with yet another apologetic look.

"Out of the question. We would never mock the devout followers of the Goddess Elazonia, especially sent from the Holy City by the Holy See itself."

"Then bring out the king!"

"As I explained, His Highness's condition is quite poor... Not to mention, haven't we already complied by allowing you to use our national treasure, the Tears of Matteral, at no cost?"

The Tears of Matteral—the Tigris Kingdom's greatest treasure—was mined from the mountains in the distant past.

Walking in and demanding they be allowed to use it for free was arrogant enough, but to demand they issue a decree that would throw their economy off the rails? No chance.

"I may be unable to keep my silence if you ask for too much," the minister warned. His easygoing manner sharpened to let through a piercing glare.

"Urgh..." The holy warrior was taken aback.

The Tigris Kingdom held complete control of the mineral-rich Matteral Mountains. Thanks to its resources, the kingdom was a large economic and military power, gathering capital from its exports and supported by toughened miners. In fact, its population had always been strong in will—due to the hardship that they endured on a day-to-day basis as miners. It was a huge mistake to think that the Tigris Kingdom would just roll over because they were up against the Goddess's church—even if they saved the lost souls, even if they resurrected and healed their true believers, even if they had the might of the undying heroes, even if they controlled other countries from behind the scenes.

"If I recall correctly, Saint Sanctina, you were sent by Cardinal Cronklum, right...? Would it be too much of an issue if I contacted Cardinal Snobe to confirm that the cardinals are in agreement with this request?"

"...*Tsk*." The holy warrior made no attempt to hide his annoyance at the mention of his name.

Cardinal Snobe was a chubby middle-aged man with a love for gold and women. None of the cardinals were cruder than him. He was also aiming for the papacy, so if he heard of their plan to use the giant magic conductor in the fight against the Demon King, he'd likely be more than happy to side with the Tigris Kingdom. As holy warriors under Cardinal Cronklum, that was an outcome they had to avoid at all costs.

"It must be more than thirty years ago, but Cardinal Snobe once worked in Tigris when he was still hunting monsters as a hero. Ever since then, the country has thought of him so fondly that we regularly send gifts of gratitude," said the minister.

"So bribes, huh? I'm not surprised," spat the holy warrior.

Both he and the minister were grinning, but there were sparks flying between them.

Sanctina jumped in with her signature smile, as if oblivious to the tense situation. "If His Highness is suffering from an illness, it is our duty as members of the church to heal him."

She was kicking herself for not realizing this sooner.

As she swiftly stood to her feet, the minister cried out in a flustered state to stop her. "Please wait. His Highness's illness has been with him from birth and cannot be healed with magic."

Right. Magic heals injuries, diseases, and any abnormalities to the person's natural state. Meaning an illness from birth would be that body's normal state. In this case, the magic wouldn't be able to locate an abnormality to heal. In the same way, magic couldn't heal aging or other natural phenomena.

When the Demon King's advisor heard this explanation, he assumed, "It uses the patient's genetic makeup to rebuild the body, but it can't change the genes themselves." Not that the minister would understand that clarification, though—much less anyone else.

"We've employed magic users in the castle as well, but even they were unable to heal His Highness..."

"Pff, those nonbelievers are half-baked magic users." One of her men snorted.

Her warriors were the cream of the crop, sought by the church when they were children for their magical potential. From a young age, they received training after training on casting healing magic. But it wasn't just their magical talents that set them apart. They had experience dissecting cadavers of who died from natural causes to help them further refine their skills.

That was the reason why your average royal mage or stray witch wouldn't be able to top the Goddess's clergy in magical attacks, let alone come close to their healing abilities.

"Wouldn't it be best for you to fire those scammers?" said another, openly sneering at the minister.

"Say all you want," replied the minister, voice rising in slight annoyance, "but am I wrong to assume you can't heal all diseases known to man?"

He was right: Magic still couldn't heal a select handful of diseases, especially if they were hereditary or genetic. In fact, the previous king had died from one of them.

The holy warrior knew better than to bring that up and add insult to injury, but he continued to taunt him without a shred of guilt. "That's what the Goddess wanted—predestined to die young. You know, I bet he was a sinner in his past life. He didn't deserve to live. That's why he was so ill from a young age."

Even with insults of his former king and trusted friend hurled at him from all directions, the minister managed to keep his cool. Inwardly, however, he cursed and spat at them. *You may act the part of holy men, but you're nothing more than incompetent, murderous bastards!*

With a firm grasp on magical cures and treatments, the Goddess's church controlled other countries by threatening their monarchs that they wouldn't be healed or resurrected if they went against the church. This was common knowledge. The news of Boar Kingdom was still fresh in the minds of the royal court in Tigris Kingdom: Their bishop was the puppeteer, coercing their king to deploy his troops against the demons in Dog Valley. Their eventual defeat was heavy in their collective consciousness.

With mounting paranoia that his kingdom would be subjected to the same fate, the previous king of Tigris Kingdom concentrated his efforts in training his royal mages—which in turn made more enemies in the church.

The minister had since suspected that the church had let the former king die for his actions. This conversation was only reinforcing his skepticism, but the Saint interrupted his thoughts, smiling sweetly.

"What kind of illness does His Highness have?"

"Hm? Uh, w-well...," he stammered, caught off guard by her question.

Observing his discomfort, she put forth her purest smile. "Perhaps his head is as cold as yours?"

"Ba-ha-ha!" Her accompanying crowd burst into loud guffaws.

It was obvious that the minister had gotten the court mage to cast an *Illusion* spell on him to create the image of such full and fluffy hair. They didn't even need to *Dispel* it to guess that he was actually as bald as an egg.

"Ha-ha-ha, I can see why the young king might hesitate to have a meeting if he suffered from the same incurable disease as you," taunted one of her warriors.

"Y-yes, he has an incurable illness like me," the minister stuttered, trembling with fury.

But he managed to crack a smile at the holy warriors as they tried to contain their laughter. Sanctina joined them all with a grin of her own before standing from the couch once again.

"We will take our leave. Please let us know as soon as His Highness feels up to a meeting."

"Take care of yourself, too," squawked another one of her men disingenuously as he theatrically cast his eyes down in pretend grief and followed the Saint out of the room.

The minister sent them off with his plastered genial smile, waiting until they'd gone a sufficient distance before kicking the couch that the Saint had sat on with all his might.

Meanwhile, Shinichi was treating some burly miners to a drink in one of the city's taverns.

"Here you go. Drink up."

"Thanks, dude."

"I dunno what kinda store you're startin' up, but I'll make sure to swing by when you're open for business."

Shinichi had told them that he was doing market research for a new store, treating them to a few drinks to hear the talk of the town. The miners had no reason not to believe him and eagerly accepted the ale.

"And so our supervisor's so damn tough on us—"

"You know, a few days ago, I was playing cards with that fatso, but man, he's so freakin' weak—like, you wouldn't believe it!"

"You know, if you want a good drink, you come here. But if you're looking for a bite to eat, you should check out The Goat's Tail over there."

"Oh yeah, cool, I see." Shinichi inserted the occasional comment or two as the miners ate, drank, and chatted away.

Once they were sufficiently drunk, he got to his real questions: "Hey, did you guys do that ritual in the cathedral? You know the one I'm talking about: beating the demons, touching that giant stone, some strange mumbo jumbo?"

As soon as he broached this topic, their faces puckered up, as if they'd taken a big chomp out of a sour lemon.

"Aw seriously, just give us a break…"

"An old hag in my neighborhood keeps naggin' me, sayin', 'You'd better go and give your devotion to the Goddess, too!' or whatever."

"Okay, but listen to this: I'd gotten a cold but couldn't take the time off work so I went to go get it healed, you know, as you do. But then I touched the stupid thing—and couldn't work *anyway*. Mom smacked me upside the head. Can you believe it?"

"I don't care if it's for the demons or whatever. It ain't got shit to do with us."

The drunker the miners got, the more extreme their complaints got.

Good, this means the average person isn't all that cooperative.

Shinichi chuckled to himself, knowing the Saint wouldn't be able to gather enough magic right away, as the miners continued to air their grievances.

"It pisses me off how high and mighty those priests act—"

"You know, they screamed their heads off, calling me 'Evil! A heretic!' or whatever—just for praying to the mountain god for a safe trip!"

"But then anytime something good happens, they're all, 'It's all thanks to our Goddess.' Cut the bullshit!"

"If their Goddess is so great, why doesn't she stop a cave-in before it happens?! But no, they're just taking a pretty little penny outta our pockets to resurrect us instead!"

"Some nerve for someone who's stolen my great-great-grandma's job."

"Hang on, I want to hear more about that!" Shinichi stopped, leaning in. Those words had caught his attention.

The miner was plastered, but he used the small remaining amount of reason in him to lower his voice. "Well, it was way before I was born. Back before the Goddess's church had spread to this country.

"Then the priests came flooding in, and it ended up like this, but there was a lot of trouble at the time. Even before the church came, we had a few people who could use a little magic or knew a lot about herbal medicines, and they'd get together and open a—what did they call it, a clinic? Some sort of shop where they'd heal people.

"Then a bunch of people from the Goddess's church went around destroying them. Used some pretty dirty methods, too.

"There's a few left here and there, like the king's healer and a couple guys hidden away in the mountains. If a store opens in the city, though, the next day it's just...*gone*, you know?"

"Yeah, I get it." Shinichi smirked, a sinister smile crawling across his face.

I was wondering why I'd never seen any medical facilities outside the church. Like, it would make sense for there to be some, but it looks like they've been using some pretty nasty tricks.

Destroy the competition and monopolize the market. Twenty-first century Japan had anti-monopoly laws in place to prevent that, but there was nothing of the sort in this world.

Seems there's still some hatred and hostility kindling in them.

If it was the time of his great-great-grandma, that must mean it was over one hundred years ago. Meaning there was no one alive from that time harboring a direct grudge, but he was sure there were some oral or written stories outlining their barbaric deeds, passed down from one generation to the next. It was like a land mine, ready to explode on the Goddess's church someday.

It's a younger religion than I thought.

Well, it spread to the Tigris Kingdom pretty slowly, which meant the church was established earlier than that. Maybe a little over two hundred years ago. He couldn't imagine it being around for one or two thousand years.

Meaning it doesn't have the history or influence that certain religions have on Earth. Especially the ones with over two billion followers.

Shinichi knew he hadn't completely understood the magnitude of the church's influence, so he couldn't let his guard down, but he felt a little better knowing it was less than he'd thought.

They all continued to chat until the miners dozed off in their drunken state, and he went to pay the owner at the counter before retiring to his room upstairs.

He smiled at the two girls waiting for him there. "Well, I've learned pretty much everything I wanted to."

"So it appears," Celes replied.

She'd listened in on the conversation using *Wire Tap*, saving him the trouble of having to explain everything.

As for the redheaded hero, Arian was sitting on the bed with her arms wrapped around her knees. This time, it wasn't out of anger or embarrassment—Arian and Celes had already made amends.

"I can't befriend anyone because of the scales on my neck, but I could've joined you downstairs and listened to the conversation, too, you know," she whined.

"That's what you're pouting over?" Shinichi let out a dry chuckle as he plopped himself down next to her. "Come on. I just told you: You need to be careful because you're pretty. You don't want some drunk guy grabbing your ass, do you? And we'd have a big problem if someone recognized you and made a scene."

"But I want to help you…"

Unlike Celes, she couldn't help him out with magic. Unlike Shinichi, she wasn't good with words. What did that make her good for? She guessed she could swing around her sword, but that wasn't useful right now.

"Not only that, I caused more problems by getting lost…," Arian muttered, burying her face in her knees, mad at herself for being so useless.

"Nah, that was Celes's fault," Shinichi consoled, and he tousled her red hair. "You're the one who told us that their iron goods were cheap and that goat meat skewers tasted good, right? And with you here, I'm not afraid of being ambushed by the church's people, you know. You make me feel safe."

"…Really?"

"Yeah, I mean, look at me. I'm a pathetic weakling, so I'm counting on you."

"Ha-ha-ha, that's not something you should tell a girl." Arian laughed. But she was so happy when he relied on her, and she pressed against his shoulder coyly.

"Shall I take my leave?" asked Celes.

"Ah?!"

Arian suddenly remembered that Celes was in the room, silent until now. Blushing fiercely, she jumped away from Shinichi.

But Celes acted like she didn't see anything, afraid that Arian would run away again if she teased her much more. "So then, what is our next move?" she asked.

"Right," Shinichi replied. "I've heard a bunch of interesting stories, but I still think it'd be best to make contact with the Saint."

Without the active cooperation of the citizens, it would take a real long time to charge the magic conductor to its full capacity. Well regardless, it didn't change the fact that this could defeat the Demon King. They needed to avoid a world war, of course, and there were a few other limitations that prevented them from just bashing in the crystal. Which meant they were left to deal with another one of those undying heroes, the Saint.

"So about making contact with her…," he started.

"Let me guess: You have no ideas?"

"No, I do have one. It's a bit cliché, you know, kinda old, lacking creativity… But I guess there's a reason it stuck around," he grumbled. It was clear he was conflicted about something as he glanced at Arian.

"What?"

"…Arian, would you help me out?"

"Huh? Like you even need to ask! Of course!"

Shinichi grabbed her shoulders to face her directly, staring into her eyes. "Even if it's something bad?"

"Yeah. I know you wouldn't do anything actually bad. I trust you."

"So you'll trust me and pretend to be the bad guy, my heel?"

She nodded. "Yeah, I'll be a bad girl for you, Shinichi…" Her cheeks flushed red from his piercing glare.

"……" Celes was thinking how the simple girl had been sweet-talked into something yet again, but she didn't say anything.

It was still early in the morning when Sanctina and her warriors trudged out of the castle. Their request to meet with the king was denied once again.

"Scampering away with some made-up illness! Those sinners!"

"We're getting nowhere with this. We should consult with Cardinal Cronklum."

"Yes," Sanctina agreed, nodding genially at the seething warriors before her.

They turned to head back to the cathedral, down a road two hundred yards from the front gate of the castle. But they halted on their tracks halfway down the alley: A dark figure had descended from the rooftops and stood in front of the group, blocking their way.

"Who are you?!" On instinct, four holy warriors stepped in front of the Saint and pointed their halberds at the silhouette.

The figure was small, covered in a black robe and veiling their face up to their eyes. It was impossible to guess their age or gender. With a sword in one hand, they shouted through the cloths in a muffled voice.

"We are the Tigris Liberation Front! Followers of the meddling Goddess, feel our wrath! For you have chased our ancestors from these lands!" they cried.

Their speech was a little awkward, definitely rehearsed, and they were trying their best to remember their lines. But the mysterious figure bolted toward the group at an impossible speed.

"You little—!"

The leading holy warrior swung his halberd, but the figure chopped its shaft in half with one swipe of their sword, sending the blade flying. With their other hand, they landed a powerful punch to his jaw.

"Gaack…!"

"Bastard!"

Once they were provoked, the two other warriors pierced their swords at their combatant at the same time, but they nimbly leaped over these blows, twisting in the air and cracking both their jaws with one sweeping kick. The remaining warrior rammed his weapon high up, aiming as they made their descent, but this challenger expertly parried the strike with their sword and planted their knee in his gut.

The four powerful holy warriors were broken and beaten, completely unable to resist as they collapsed. It all happened so quickly and marvelously that the passersby forgot to scream in terror.

In the middle of the quiet street and without her holy men, Sanctina finally spoke an incantation, a beat late. *"Fireball."*

"—?!"

The combatant's eyes were wide open in shock, gaping at the three-foot flame. This spell should have invoked a fire the size of a watermelon. But that wasn't what they were gawking at.

We're in the middle of town! Why would you put the people around us in danger?

What would the Saint do if her target dodged, and the sphere exploded in the vicinity?

After that fleeting moment of indecision, the figure raised their sword above their head. As their magic power surged and passed through their body, they put all their might into striking the approaching *Fireball.*

"Hyaah!" The sword slashed into it, faster than the speed of sound, and split the ball in two.

The blow sent a shock wave to the surrounding area, scattering away the remaining halves into millions of tiny sparks and flames.

With an invisible wall shielding the crowd, the fluttering sparks were blocked from singeing a single onlooker.

"Brilliant white, pure and holy lightning—" Sanctina began, calling an even more powerful spell. But her assailant bolted toward her, their glinting sword swinging up, about to cut through her body.

"Watch out!"

From the side, a new silhouette flew in, catching the attack with his sword. "My lovely lady. Were you injured?"

It was a handsome blond boy, a faint smile playing across his face—a knight in shining armor.

Sanctina flashed him a sweet smile and replied: "—pierce my enemies, *Call Lightning*."

She didn't care at all.

"...What?"

Behind the boy, who just stood there dumbfounded, the sky flooded and unleashed lightning onto her attacker.

"Aaah!"

With a magic barrier hastily thrown up around them at the last minute, the lightning seemed to dwindle in size as it forced its way through.

But even then, the bolt was still strong, zapping the figure and causing them to let out shrieks of pain, as patches of their robe smoldered from the heat. There didn't seem to be any serious damage to the person.

"What's happening out here?!" cried some soldiers who'd been guarding the castle.

When the assailant saw them approaching, they bounded high onto the rooftops of the buildings nearby and hurriedly made their escape.

"...My lady. Were you injured?" The blond boy tried again, finally snapping back to his senses now that this chaotic scene was over.

Sanctina nodded as she showed him a bright-white smile. "I'm fine. Thank you for saving me."

"Oh, it was nothing. But I don't think these guys have given up. If you'd like, I could protect—"

"Excuse me. I must be going now." She bowed and turned on her heel before he could finish delivering his lines.

"Hey, wait a second!" he called after her as she walked over to heal the four fallen warriors and head back to the cathedral together. "......"

"Can I ask you about what happened?" One of the royal soldiers patted his shoulder as if to cheer him up.

"…Sure."

With a whole bunch of witnesses at the scene of the attack, the blond boy wasn't their prime suspect, and they let him go after some basic questioning.

He set off, trying to put distance between himself and the cathedral. Once he was satisfied, he stepped into the shadows of some buildings and took off the blond wig.

"Well that strategy was a failure," Shinichi remarked as he sighed and stuffed the wig in his bag. It had set him back three whole coins.

Two girls approached him.

"She didn't even acknowledge you," Celes commented, expressionless.

"Ah well. Nothing we can do about it!" Arian added cheerfully, happy that she didn't need to compete with any more girls for Shinichi. *Whew. No new rivals this time…*

It goes without saying that Celes directed the whole thing behind the scenes and Arian played the part of the black-robed assailant.

"Arian, were you hurt?" Shinichi asked.

"Nah, I'm fine since Celes was protecting me!"

"You're tough," Celes sighed, admiring and skeptical of Arian's ability to bounce back from those attacks.

That kind of lightning would have fried her body if she were any old human being.

"That didn't work at all," he lamented, giving up this plan for good.

"It seems that way," said Celes, making no attempt to reprimand him.

With Arian playing the part of a terrorist, the plan was for Shinichi to swoop in and save the Saint to get closer to her: the "*Ba-dum!* My Knight in Shining Armor" strategy. A classic.

But it completely fell apart when she brusquely brushed him aside. They weren't frustrated that their plan failed, however. They were struck by how strange the Saint was.

"Someone saves your life and you just keep casting your magic? Not even a thanks? Is she a robot or something?"

"I don't know what a robot is, but it was strange."

"Yeah, and she hurled attack magic without considering the danger to people around us…," whispered Arian.

If Arian had dodged the attack instead of splitting the Fireball—and if Celes hadn't thrown up a barrier at that exact moment—the onlookers could have been seriously injured—or even killed. Of course, these wounds could be cured and the dead resurrected, so maybe the Saint was right to throw these spells without hesitation. But humans were emotional creatures, weren't they? They didn't make judgments on logic alone.

"I mean, not only did she endanger your average Joes, she also didn't seem too fond of a boy who saved her life… Is she emotionless?" He immediately shook his head in disagreement with himself. "No, that's not it. It's not that she doesn't have emotions. It's that she doesn't *see* other people."

"Doesn't see other people?" Arian asked.

"Her eyes perceive other people, obviously. And she can reply when others talk to her. But she has no real interest or consideration. She looks at humans the same way she looks at the pebbles under her feet… At least, that's the feeling I got," Shinichi explained.

He shivered slightly as he remembered the look in the Saint's eyes as she looked up at him: clear and sharp, befitting of a Saint, and completely empty, like glass orbs. Thinking back, she'd smiled gently at the followers as they gave their power to the magic conductor, but there didn't seem to be an ounce of gratitude in her heart.

"I know some people who love everyone so much that it makes them indifferent to each individual. But to me, her indifference makes her look like she loves all people, even though she clearly doesn't."

No nepotism or special treatment. She treated everyone the same. At first glance, this made her saintly. At second glance, this meant she didn't love anyone.

"Is she truly indifferent or just acting like it...? Either way, what would catch her eye? Or who?"

All he had was questions. Completely at a loss, he just couldn't understand the Saint.

After all, he was just a high-school student, no matter how clever he was for his age. In his seventeen years of existence, he'd never met a beast like her, one who had been taken into the church as a child and drilled day and night with the Goddess's teachings—the best kind of pawn.

"...It's useless. I just don't get it." Shinichi slumped, looking at Celes with a big sigh. "There isn't some magic to see someone's emotions or thoughts, is there?"

"If you mean *Mind Reading*, yes, but I would not recommend it."

"Why?"

"Because you need to touch the other person in order to read their mind. And they immediately become aware that you're looking at their thoughts the moment you touch them. Plus, you can only read their superficial thoughts, the ones on the very surface."

She explained that if you dived too deeply into their mind, you risked psychological destruction as your thoughts and their thoughts mixed and blurred the lines.

"That won't work, then..."

"What shall we do next?"

"Well, for now, we'll put a pin in the 'get close to the Saint'-type strategies."

There was no way he could make a romantic, friendly, or any kind of relationship with a monster whose thought processes he couldn't understand at all. After coming to that conclusion, he thought furiously for a few minutes before announcing his decision.

"All right, full speed ahead to the Demon King's castle!"

"Woo!" exclaimed Arian.

"We're just running away, aren't we?" Celes clarified.

The three chose to attack by dashing away from their opponent—in other words, a tactical withdrawal—and left the Tigris Kingdom for the time being.

As Celes teleported them back to the castle, Rino and the Demon King waited for the three after they received news with *Telepathy* that they were coming home.

"Welcome home, Shinichi!" Rino exclaimed, trotting up to him happily.

"I'm home," he replied, grabbing her sides and lifting her high in the air.

"Did you come home just to play?" joked Celes in her usual sarcastic tone, as she brought out the meat skewers that she'd gotten to go.

"Oh, Rino, you have it all…," Arian whispered, looking a bit jealous as Shinichi lifted Rino in the air.

"And? Any progress?" asked the Demon King.

"Not much," Shinichi reported. With a bitter expression on his face, he informed the King of the Saint and the magic conductor.

"A magic conductor taller than me, huh? That might just do me in!"

"That's not something you should be happy about, *remember*? Anyway, I can't think of a good plan, so I figured I'd ask the dwarves for some info."

"Of course, there are none more knowledgeable than dwarves when it comes to stone and metal." The King agreed with a nod, then led them all to the basement.

Lower, lower, and far lower than his training room, there was a workshop so deep underground that the sun's rays would never penetrate its inky blackness. In that damp room was a creature no taller than Shinichi's waist, strapped with heavy muscle, who had blackish-blue skin, a white beard, and a round belly like a keg of ale. This was the demons' blacksmith, a dwarf.

"Worthless again!" he bellowed, taking no notice of them as they slipped into the workshop. Instead, he threw the sword he'd just forged down to the ground with a clang.

"Hard at work, I see, Ivan," the Demon King called toward him.

"Your Highness?!" he yelped in surprise. Ivan the dwarf was flustered as he knelt in front of the King. "My deepest apologies! I still have not been able to forge a blade capable of winning against your fists!"

"Ha-ha, no need to rush. Just keep moving forward." The King laughed, encouraging him, as tears of shame flowed freely down the dwarf's face.

"I'm weirded out about not being weirded out by *a blade capable of winning against fists*," Shinichi remarked.

"Too late for that now," Celes quipped.

She gestured to the mountain of broken swords in the corner of the workshop. Every single one was bent out of shape. Broken in battle against the great Demon King. A pile of spent corpses.

"This is— Are these all magic swords?!" Arian cried as she tiptoed up to the pile out of curiosity, pulling out a broken blade.

To test it out, she swung the fragment at the solid stone wall. And sure enough, it sliced through the stone like clay.

"But even that's not good enough…"

"Hm, girly, yeah, you with the red hair," Ivan called out. "Aren't you that hero who injured His Highness?"

"Yeah, but…" Arian hesitated, nodding in terror that he resented her.

But the dwarf walked up to her with an excited expression. "Exactly what kind of sword did you use?! Was it iron? Or steel? How many times was it folded?"

"Umm, it was iron and thick and sturdy. Nothing fancy…"

"Hmm, wouldn't that shatter easily if used against His Highness?"

"Yeah, that's why I put magic into it through the handle to make it harder."

Arian used the broken sword to demonstrate. The light that flowed from her hand into the sword had a similar effect to an *Enchanted Weapon* spell, significantly strengthening and improving the cutting edge of the sword.

When she swung at the wall for the second time, it sliced through it smoothly like water.

"Oh, huh. Makes sense why you wouldn't think to buy a more expensive weapon," Shinichi said, finally realizing why she'd used a cheap iron sword for so long.

Next to him, however, the dwarf slouched his shoulders in disappointment. "So the wielder was the one who was exceptional. Well, this doesn't help me at all."

"But you can make such lovely magic swords. Please don't be upset...," Arian begged, trying to console him as he shook his head dejectedly.

Shinichi watched the two as he plucked the rejected sword from the floor, the one the dwarf had thrown down in frustration earlier. "Why don't I feel any magic power or spells from it at all? I mean, isn't it called a magic sword for that reason?"

"Son, you're just stating the obvious," replied the dwarf, as if this was common knowledge. "You cast magic on these swords to make them harder, sharper, while you forge them to make the most superior blade. It doesn't mean they have magic power or spells in them."

"What, *seriously*?!" cried Shinichi, astounded that it was completely different from the "magic swords" in his favorite fantasy RPGs. "You all kept saying 'magic sword this' and 'magic sword that,' so I assumed you had cool stuff like The Unbreakable Sword or The Infinite Fireballs Sword or something..."

"I wouldn't be working so hard if that were the case!" he retorted, indignant.

"Really... Huh, well, if I think about it logically, I guess that'd be impossible."

To be honest, Shinichi was a little disappointed by this revelation, but he understood why this was the case. To break something down, you would need to apply some kind of energy to its surface, whether it be hitting it or burning it, to break the bonds between the molecules. In order to make something completely indestructible, you'd have to make it so that energy never reached it from the outside. That meant taking it out of time and space: You would need to freeze time or put it in another dimension.

It might be possible for the Demon King to wield this magic for a moment, but it would be impossible to sustain it for an eternity.

As for the Infinite Fireballs Sword, well, it would have to be able to put out infinite amounts of energy, which went totally against the laws of thermodynamics.

Of course, it'd be a whole different story if the magic tool contained a universe of infinite resources or a wormhole to another dimension where it could steal that energy.

"It would've been so fun to make a thermal power plant using the Infinite Fireballs Sword and achieve the cleanest energy known to man..."

"You lost me," Rino whined, unable to understand his grand ideas. After all, they associated electricity with lightning in their world.

"To recap: You can make super-hard, super-sharp swords just by casting magic on them, right? Even though they don't store any magical power or spells?"

"Righty-ho," the dwarf confirmed.

"Which means...you're changing the structure or arrangement of the atoms?"

Was it similar to his *Element Conversion* spell?

The dwarf's eyes flashed with interest. "What do ya mean?"

"Right, well... To start, all matter is made up of a collection of atoms, tiny little particles."

"So that's what they're called. Atoms. Didn't know the name, but I know what you're talking about: When you break down a stone, it turns into sand."

"And you know what coal and diamonds are, right? Well, both of those are made from the same type of atom, carbon."

"WHAT?!"

"If they're made from the same source, how can their appearances be so different? And their hardness? That all comes down to how the atoms are connected," Shinichi explained as he plucked a piece of charcoal from a nearby desk and drew a diagram on the floor.

"You see, the atoms in coal are arranged haphazardly. That's why it's weak enough to crumble with even the smallest amount of pressure. On the other hand, diamonds have atoms that are arranged in an organized grid-like pattern, making it the hardest substance in the world."

"Hmmm..."

"In the same way, iron and other metals are structured almost randomly. But I've heard if you make the arrangement more rigid, like diamonds, you could theoretically make a super-metal."

"Is this true?!"

"Well, theoretically, yes. But my world hasn't found a way to make it yet. If we were in zero gravity—," Shinichi started to say, but the rest of his words never reached the dwarf's ears.

"Tiny particles, aligning atoms, orderly arrangement... This! This is the magic I've needed!"

Magic is "a way to alter reality to match your imagination." This is what Celes's teacher said. The clearer your imagination, the more effective the magic is.

There was a huge difference in wishing vaguely for a "harder sword" and specifically visualizing a "sword in a neat atomic grid." This otherworldly knowledge pierced through the foggy limitations of the dwarf's mind like a beam of light.

He let out a joyous bellow as he grasped his hammer. "This time! This time, I will surpass His Highness's fists—!"

He was still laughing as he started a fire, preparing to make a new sword.

Shinichi recoiled a little, weirded out, as Celes whispered in his ear. "So we came here to excite Sir Ivan?"

"Ah, I almost forgot!"

Just like any normal boy, he'd gotten so delirious with excitement learning about this entire process that he forgot to ask his original question.

"Sorry, Ivan, before you get to work, I was hoping you could tell us a bit about magic conductors."

"Hmph, just when I got in the groove of things… But it would be wrong if I didn't show my gratitude to my muse."

After all, he was indebted to Shinichi, and it would be dishonorable to shoot down his question. Shinichi explained their situation so far.

"A massive magic conductor?" asked Ivan. "I want one, too."

"Right? It could be used as a magic bomb, sure, but what if it generated enough energy to—"

"You are getting off topic again," Celes reminded, interrupting as the blacksmith dwarf and science nerd chatted excitedly, eyes gleaming.

"Okay, am I right to think of magic conductors as some sort of magic storage tank?"

"That's right," confirmed the dwarf with a nod. He walked off to bring a small crystal out from the back corner. It was hardly the size of a marble. And though its size obviously fell very short of the one in Tigris Kingdom, it gleamed and sparkled in the exact same way.

"This is it. It's also known as a 'stone leech.' If you're good with this size, you can find this junk anywhere if you take a moment to mine in the demon world."

"Hmm, not exactly rare, huh?"

"Might be rare in the human world. I dunno," he offered.

Shinichi took a second to admire it. In that moment, the dwarf pressed the magic conductor into Shinichi's open palm with his gloved hand.

The moment he touched the stone, he turned icy cold, as if it stole all his warmth. At the same time, his magic power pulsed into the crystal.

"Ah! So that's what it's like to have your magic sucked out."

"It's not a serious problem with a stone that size," the dwarf confirmed.

"I bet I'd be fine with twenty more."

That said, it wasn't a fun sensation, kinda like having your blood drained by force.

The crystal glowed with a pale light that was both beautiful and a little off-putting, uncanny.

"Now that it's charged up, try to pull the magic back out and cast a spell," Ivan instructed.

"Pull the magic back out...*Light*."

Shinichi concentrated hard, forming the image in his mind. This time, he felt the energy surging in the opposite direction—heat was flowing into him. The moment the spell was complete and illuminated their surroundings, the small crystal shattered into a million pieces.

"Sorry, I think I broke it."

"Don't worry about it. It was impure anyway. A shitty one." The dwarf laughed as he held out a trash can. "Just like that. You can store magic in it now and use it later."

"Seems convenient."

But then, why hadn't Arian seen one before? Why didn't Celes know more about them?

Ivan replied to his internal questions, shaking his head back and forth. "They're not. Even if you put magic into one, it holds it about a day before it disappears."

"Wait, it doesn't store it forever?!"

"If this piece of rock was that useful, it wouldn't earn the name 'stone leech.'" The dwarf clicked his tongue as he recalled a bad memory. "There have been many times where I was mining for iron or silver and hit these instead. They'd drain my energy and make it so I'd have to put a halt to my work. Frustrating, to say the least."

"But you've kept some of them."

"As long as you don't touch them with your bare hands, you're fine.

You can use them in place of quartz to make certain objects. And if you cast the same spell over and over onto a magic conductor that's really pure, it can activate the same magic spell by sucking out some magic power. It's a process called imprinting."

Using this process, they made lamps all around the castle containing the *Light* spell.

"Many of the lanterns were made by Sir Ivan," Celes added.

"They'd explode if I touched them, so Celestia provides magic power to get them to light up."

"I help sometimes, too!" exclaimed Rino.

"Oh, good girl," Shinichi praised, tousling her hair as she adorably puffed her chest in pride.

He took another glance at the fragments of the magic conductor in the trash can. "How long can it hold on to magic before it fades away?"

"Depends on the size," Ivan answered. "That shitty little stone right there could hold on to it for half a day, tops. But that massive magic conductor? Maybe two months."

"Two months, huh? Not too bad." The corners of his mouth tugged into a fiendish smirk.

If it could store magic indefinitely, then it wouldn't be impossible for a single Saint to defeat the Demon King, given time. But with a two-month expiration date? Shinichi could think of a more than a handful of ways to interfere with their progress.

"Is that all? If so, I need to focus. Please take your leave," Ivan requested.

"Yeah, thanks for your help."

With Ivan in quiet concentration, his back turned to them, they all strolled out of the workshop after they expressed their gratitude.

"Were you able to think of a new strategy?" Celes asked.

"I'm getting there." Shinichi nodded as he gathered his thoughts.

They couldn't destroy the giant magic conductor for fear of inciting war with the humans. It would be near impossible to persuade the

Saint to become allies, considering she had absolutely no interest in them. A number of problems were running through his head as he looked at Arian, then Celes, and finally stopped to look at Rino.

"What is it, Shinichi?" the Demon King's daughter asked.

"Your Highness, I have a question," he said, ignoring her question for now. He voiced his final concern: "How do you tell demons and humans apart?"

"Come again? Look and you can see."

Why are you asking me this now? his look of exasperation seemed to say.

But Shinichi's smile only got wider. "So outside of appearance, there's no way to tell the two apart? There's no *Search* magic or something that only activates for demons?"

"If there are any, I'm unfamiliar with them, at least."

"Celes?"

"I've never had a need for such magic, so I've never tried to learn it."

"Arian?"

"Umm, well, until recently, I only though they existed in fairy tales, so I've never heard of anything like that."

His grin grew and grew as he listened to their three answers, until finally, he clapped a hand on Rino's shoulder. Yes, Rino, a demonic beauty—pure-white skin and ruby eyes. No horns, no tail, not a single feature that would give her away as a demon.

"Rino, I'm gonna make you into an idol! You're gonna be a star!"

"An idol?" Rino asked. "What's that?"

As a true star in the making, she delivered her final line—"Can you eat it?"—taking her first steps on the long and treacherous road to idoldom.

Chapter 3
The Singing Princess from the Demon World
and the Dirty Way to Do Business

"You are the chosen children."

This was Sanctina's first memory.

She was born and raised in the children's home that Cardinal Cronklum ran as part of his charity work—well, it was actually a factory for creating pawns, loyal to him and the church. She'd been told that her parents had abandoned her—when in reality, a pair of beautiful, powerful magic users were paid off to create her.

They might not have totally understood genetics in this world yet, but they'd noticed that children seemed to inherit their parents' traits. At the very least, they understood it was more likely these magic users would make beautiful, powerful boys and girls.

At the time, Cronklum was already a cardinal, already aiming for papacy. He needed a symbol to capture the people's hearts—something prepossessing and magnificent, something to improve his image. That's why he created and raised five children, including Sanctina.

"Look, normal children can't use magic," said the serene middle-aged woman who ran the house as she jabbed a finger toward the kids outside passing by. "But you've all been chosen by the Goddess. That's why you can use magic from birth."

Rumor had it she was Cronklum's lover.

The clerical staff under Cronklum cast *Protection* and other spells on all the children over and over again. Sanctina's magic power had developed enough that she was taking her first steps into the realm of magic at the young age of five.

"Magic is the way our Goddess professes her love for you. Work hard to make her love you even more."

"Yes, ma'am!" All the children eagerly agreed with their caretaker, casting magic on one another until they collapsed from exhaustion.

She thought about one particular day, an incident where one of the five children sneaked out of the home. She was brought back crying, saying she'd wanted to meet her real parents.

When the caretaker heard her story, she reprimanded her, quietly but firmly. "As a child loved by the Goddess, you're her child. Don't be led astray by blood. Focus on giving your love to the Goddess."

The other four children were in earnest agreement, but this little runaway wasn't placated by these words. Just a few days later, she ran away from the home for the second time.

After she'd been caught by the holy warriors, she was never seen again.

"She just didn't have enough love for the Goddess," their caretaker lamented. But she didn't tell them what had become of her.

The other children soon forgot all about the girl, losing themselves in their magic practice.

On the day of Sanctina's twelfth birthday, the four children were taken to the Archbasilica. There, in front of Cronklum and his crew, they knelt in front of the statue of the Goddess.

"This body, this power, I give it all to our Goddess Elazonia. I swear to continue the fight against those who threaten peace on this world."

They participated in the ceremony for receiving the Goddess's blessing to become an undying hero.

On that day, there were only two children who were accepted by the Goddess: Sanctina and a young boy, both branded by the symbol of the sun.

The other two were powerful magic users and became priests, sent to remote villages to spread the word of the Goddess. But Sanctina didn't know what happened to them after that.

"You are the chosen heroes. Do good," cried the caretaker, wiping the tears from her eyes as she sent them off.

They were sent to Cronklum after that. Up until then, they'd only seen him in between his official duties, but he invited them into his mansion with a welcoming smile.

But their day-to-day changed little from their time at the children's home. During the day, they focused on training their magic abilities. At night, they read the holy book and reflected on their faith in the Goddess. Every once in a while, Cronklum would order them to accompany the holy warriors to a nearby village to blast away a ravaging monster. This routine was on constant repeat.

When Sanctina defeated a giant centipede monster, the villagers lined up and thanked her, hot tears running down their faces.

"Heroes, thank you so much."

"I was worried we would be annihilated if it weren't for you. I can't express my gratitude."

"Miss, thank you for saving us!"

To Sanctina, a monster that would've made mincemeat of a group of average magic users was nothing more than a sewer rat. Such were her magical abilities. But to those who weren't undying heroes or even particularly skilled warriors, these beasts were so great a threat that they had no choice but to abandon their homes, pack up, and flee.

But Sanctina couldn't understand the weight of their decisions. At the children's home, she never once experienced extreme hunger or cold. She couldn't even begin to imagine that by choosing to abandon their tilled fields, the villagers were proclaiming they'd rather save their lives than their livelihoods.

But as the crowd fussed over her, exalting their praise, she experienced an unfamiliar sensation—something rippling through her heart, making its way down her body.

"Please pay no mind. It was my duty as a hero," she said to them.

"Oh, so generous!"

"A noble heart! You must be the reincarnation of the Goddess Elazonia."

"Our hero… No, no, our Saint!"

They threw themselves on the ground in front of her in reverence at the sight of her heavenly smile. Tales of the incident spread from town to town, and Sanctina started to be recognized as the Saint.

At around the same time, the other hero was brooding, starting to become more turbulent and out of control.

"A Saint? Gimme a break. Don't be so full of yourself," he spat, hurling abuse and taunts her way.

But Sanctina couldn't understand why he was so full of rage and fury: his inferiority complex, her matchless magical capacity and gorgeous looks, his plain appearance, his secret love and lust for her.

And then one day, he attacked her, tried to force himself on her, as she was bathing in her room. She managed to fend him off, blasting him through the air with an attack spell, before anything too serious could happen between them. But after careful consideration, Cronklum decided to remove the boy from his residence. And he disappeared without a trace. Even to this day, she didn't know whatever happened to this other undying hero.

All she knew was from that moment on, Sanctina wasn't one of five chosen children or one of two heroes anymore. She was the one and only Saint.

"You are the chosen one. Remember to carry yourself in a way befitting a Saint."

"Yes, Cardinal Cronklum."

Sanctina nodded as her face melted into a saintly smile, saturated with tender love.

But there was some other emotion brewing behind her smile, something that Sanctina couldn't exactly put her finger on.

It had been ten days since Saint Sanctina and her holy warriors had come to the mining country of Tigris. Ten days, and yet to be granted a meeting with the king.

"I can't take this anymore. Let them experience our might! Our power!"

All thirty holy warriors were gathered in the prayer room, venting their outrage in collective synchronicity.

"We'll never defeat those deviant monsters if the King's being all stingy and uncooperative."

"We're losing traction, and the number of people visiting the cathedral has dropped these past few days. We've got to get a decree out."

"We'll unleash the true extent of her rage on them!"

"Please. Let's not stir things up…," protested a meek voice.

It was the fifty-year-old bishop stationed in the Cathedral of Tigris Kingdom.

Going back a hundred years ago, their missionaries had done some heinous things to the healers and medicine makers in the kingdom. To this day, their people held a certain amount of resentment toward the church. Despite that, the bishop had been able to handle the situation fairly well, without causing any serious issues.

It would fare really badly for him if the warriors were to reignite old flames.

But it was obvious they looked down on him; they made no attempt to hide their derision at his timid, demure nature.

"Don't be ridiculous. An insult against us is an insult against the Goddess. We will fail as her humble servants if we choose to let it go."

"Th-that may be so, but…," the bishop stammered.

In any other case, he should have been their superior. But since they reported directly to Cardinal Cronklum, these lines were blurred, as the cardinal granted them more authority and influence than the average bishop. He couldn't resist or object too strongly.

In the middle of all that commotion, Sanctina had been sitting silently with her eyes closed.

She suddenly stood up. "I've received a telepathic message from Cardinal Cronklum."

"Oh, finally!"

In a previous report, she'd already explained to Cronklum that the royal palace lent them the Tears of Matteral but denied them a meeting with their king. This had put a halt to their progress.

Upon hearing this news, Cronklum set forth a few plans of his own—giving money to other cardinals, pulling some strings behind the scenes, working this way and that. His work had finally paid off: The stage was now set.

"And?" asked one of the holy warriors in haste. "What kind of punishment will the Archdiocese hand down?"

"Until His Highness cooperates," she started with a grin, "the people will need to donate five times more to be healed from disease, and the act of resurrection will be strictly prohibited."

"Oooh, wonderful!"

"What?! Impossible!" cried the bishop through their applause and cheers. His face rapidly drained of all color.

He didn't even want to imagine the riots and rebellions erupting across town in light of this news. Mining accidents happened day in and day out. If they surged the prices on healing and got rid of resurrection altogether, he knew violence and chaos would ensue for sure.

Even before it came to that, he would have to inform tearstained family members and loved ones of the deceased that sure, they had ways to resurrect them, but sorry, no can do. What was he supposed to say? *Just let 'em rot into soil*? That would be inhumane.

"I don't care *how* much His Highness's actions upset you. As followers of the Goddess, don't you think—" the bishop pleaded, objecting desperately.

"We'll do anything to exterminate those foul creatures. *That's* her divine will!"

They lowered their halberds toward him, forcing him to silence. But he continued to resist wordlessly.

Sanctina turned to him. "Bishop, I have a message for you from Cardinal Cronklum." She flashed him a smile. "Starting today, you and your attendants will be reassigned to the Cathedral of the Boar Kingdom."

"What in the—?!" shrieked the elderly bishop at his reassignment. "This can't be! It's been rumored that the cathedral hasn't even been rebuilt, that there is a mountain of incomplete resurrections: the fallen soldiers, the clergy killed under its rubble…"

"Yes. Cardinal Cronklum is entrusting you with those tasks." Another innocent smile.

It made the bishop dizzy, breaking his resolve.

He'd heard that the king of Boar Kingdom was intelligent, albeit spineless. And yet, he'd turned Hube in, reported his transgression to the Holy See. That's how much the king resented Hube, how much anger he still held against the church.

His task was to go there, resurrect heaps of people day after day, on top of healing the injured and ill, on top of gathering the funds necessary to rebuild the cathedral. It was a roundabout way of saying "I hope you die from physical and mental exhaustion."

"Why would he…?"

The bishop hadn't lined his own pockets or taken advantage of his position or engaged in obscene acts. He'd worked diligently through all his suffering, fulfilling his duties to the church. Why was he being punished for his efforts?

His only so-called crime was that he was unable to sacrifice innocent people for the good of the church and Holy See and that he had too honest a personality. But even that was a stretch.

There was evidence of this when the previous king collapsed two years ago. He wasn't favored by the church by any means. The bishop gave his professional opinion as a healer that the church should heal the king with their secret methods. But that advice wasn't appropriate for his role as a member of the Goddess's church. The cardinals had been irritated by his suggestion.

He bemoaned the ridiculousness of this entire situation. The holy warriors yanked him off his feet and dragged him out of the prayer room.

All the while, Sanctina just kept smiling and smiling.

If the highest authority in the church ordered it done, then it needed to be done. She knew that much as a follower of the Goddess—and as a Saint.

"I pray for your success from the bottom of my heart," she called after the bishop as he was punted out of the cathedral.

She wasn't lying. But she also didn't specify whom she was addressing.

"Well then," she said. "Let us deliver Cardinal Cronklum's orders to the castle."

"I hope we can meet His Perpetually Ill Highness instead of his little baldy minister."

As they walked toward the castle, the warriors continued to make snide remarks and laughed boisterously the entire way.

The church strictly forbade all resurrections and inflated the price of healing by five times, until all citizens of the Tigris Kingdom cooperated with their mission to fill the Tears of Matteral.

They were to destroy all remaining clinics in the city. The people would riot upon hearing this news.

But their enemy was an undying hero, capable of wielding the most powerful spells known to humankind—Saint Sanctina.

With a sweep of her hand, she could slaughter thousands of ordinary people at once. If they managed to kill her, she would be resurrected every time. There was no way they would be able to push her back.

With enough time, she could annihilate the tens of thousands of people in the Tigris Kingdom if it came down it. There was nothing to gain from fighting this beast.

That left them with one option: bend to the church's will and surrender to her rule.

With spite pinching and piercing their every word, the holy warriors explained this situation to the minister. He nodded with a look of pain but didn't stand from his spot on the sofa.

"...I will consult with His Highness. Please go for today."

"Fine. But remember: This is effective immediately."

"I sure hope His Highness gets better before it's too late."

They hurled their irritation and displeasure at him without mercy, airing out their pent-up rage. The minister, they thought, deserved it.

"Well then, we await His Highness's response," Sanctina announced, her perpetual smile plastered on her face as she stood and left the meeting room.

And with that, Tigris Kingdom surrendered to the Goddess's church and offered their loyal subjects and their magical power—or so they thought.

"...They're not coming."

It was already past noon, the day after their warning. Not a single royal messenger had visited the cathedral.

What's more, there were no injured or ill patients in sight. They'd all stopped coming to the cathedral—totally dropped off, zip, zero, zilch.

Well, sure, they had put a sign outside yesterday, outlining the price increases and newly prohibited treatments, and they'd certainly expected to see a decrease in the number of visitors. But not like this. It was odd that there was no one here to see them at all.

On top of that, the cathedral was completely empty, save for a few zealous devotees.

In the prayer room, everyone was dumbfounded, shaking their heads and trying to make sense of the situation.

At that moment, one of the younger holy warriors came whizzing in. "W-we've got some trouble!"

"What happened? What's gotten you so worked up?"

"Someone is healing people! In the city!"

"What?!"

The holy warriors' faces stiffened in light of this news. Treating patients was the church's specialty—and a major source of their income.

Even during normal circumstances, they wouldn't allow someone to edge into their territory. And they'd just changed their policies to make their bratty king fold. If the city became overrun with unaffiliated healers, the people would start to realize they didn't need the church in the first place.

"It can't be someone acting under the king, can it?"

"No. I think it's an ordinary citizen. No relation to the king. When I asked around, I heard they appeared suddenly, a few days ago..."

"Either way, we can't just let them be! Go stop them! Now!"

"Yes, understood," Sanctina affirmed.

With the warriors worked up and by her side, she left the church, following the young messenger to an area away from the city proper, right next to the city walls.

This was where the troops were in standby during war. It was a wide area, no buildings in sight. There was usually no one there, other than the occasional group of children playing ball. But at the moment, there were throngs of people asking to get their wounds or illnesses treated.

"Okay. Get in line. No pushing."

"We're prioritizing those with serious injuries first. Please step aside and wait in those chairs if you're hoping to treat a minor wound!"

There was a pair directing the crowd: a boy with black hair and an energetic girl in a hat and glasses. At the very front of the line, a young girl of arresting beauty, treating the injured. She looked no older than ten.

"Pain, pain, fly away, *Full Healing.*"

She was healing a blood-splattered man with a gaping puncture wound, attacked by some monster in the mountains, no doubt. A light flickered and flooded from her glowing palm, swirling and surrounding his arm. The wound sealed up before their eyes and color settled back onto his pale face.

"Wow! No more pain!" he exulted, swinging his arm this way and that to test its condition. With gratitude, he squeezed her hand tightly. "Thank you so much, Miss Rino, no, *Lady* Rino!"

"I'm happy you feel better, too, mister." Rino grinned from ear to ear.

"No need to pay. Please move ahead. We have a long line behind you," quipped a maid from behind.

She was wearing a long cap that covered her ears. She directed the man to get a move on and called the next in line.

The holy warriors couldn't believe their eyes.

"Seriously? Isn't she too young to be performing magic this difficult?!"

"What does that matter? Why aren't they taking money for it?!"

After the treatment was complete, the patients expressed their thanks. Not a single silver coin changed hands. And no one pressed them to pay.

"Impossible. They won't make a profit this way..."

Well, not exactly the kind of words you'd expect to hear from her humble servants. But it was their honest-to-goodness impression.

Against a backdrop of stunned holy warriors, a group of miners rushed forward, carrying a wooden plank with an outstretched body.

"Somebody help us! We have someone crushed in a cave-in!"

He was still a boy. His neck was twisted in a crude, unnatural way, crushed by falling stones and bent horribly out of shape.

As she stepped forward with the maid, the young girl showed no disgust or discomfort at the sight of the lifeless body. Her little fingers wrapped around the maid's hand to borrow some of her magic as she chanted a certain incantation.

It was for a spell that bishops and other high-ranking officials could cast with some difficulty.

"Everyone is waiting for you, please open your eyes, *Resurrection*."

A blinding light blasted out to cocoon the corpse as his neck gently turned back to its place. He slowly blinked open his eyes.

"No. Freaking. Way. This girl can resurrect people…?!"

In front of the holy warriors, the group of miners excitedly hugged the boy, warmly welcoming him back. The men were frozen in place. They couldn't understand how this was happening.

For any living creature, their greatest fear was death. The ability to turn that back, to resurrect the dead, was one of the pillars of the church's faith.

They looked on their newfound enemy with wonder. She was making all the residents reconsider the value, the meaning of the church.

"What do we do? We can't *not* eliminate her."

"But it'll end badly if we try anything in front of all these people."

She was basically the savior to the people, coming to their rescue the moment the church halted their normal operations. If they let on that they hurt her, the people would freak out and attack them.

Of course, they could easily fend them off. But if news of a slaughter reached the king's ears, their veiled ruler would explode in unbridled rage, waging a full-blown war against the church for sure.

With the help of their undying heroes, the church would never lose such a war. That said, normal nonheroes—like the holy warriors, your average believers, their friends and families—would be destroyed beyond hope for resurrection in the counterattack. Even if these men had blind faith in their church, they were still people. They still put their lives first. They were still afraid to die.

"For now, we'll wait until everyone has gone."

"By the way, what's that?" The young holy warrior pointed behind the young girl to a wooden platform, kind of like a performing-arts stage. "And what are those people doing?"

He was talking about the group of men in strange outfits, standing a little ways away. Their eyes were sparkling in anticipation.

Beyond that, a crowd—healed patients, their accompanying family members, the local children—was starting to gather, waiting for something to start.

"What exactly is going on?" The holy warriors glared in their direction in suspicion.

The crowd was growing more and more excited with each passing second.

They were waiting expectantly, patiently, for the right moment, to see something totally new, something unimaginable, something to light up their very souls.

The black-haired boy organizing the patients into neat lines was Shinichi. When he saw Rino start to breathe more heavily, panting, he called out to the crowds of people.

"Okay, that's all the healings for today! If you don't have a life-threatening condition, please come back again tomorrow!"

"Whaaat?!"

The people in the line groaned in disappointment, but none showed anger. After all, the healings were free. They didn't have a right to be irritated—in fact, most of them were just grateful. Besides, they knew that if they made a scene, they'd be sent away and miss the main event of the day.

There was one troublemaker who didn't know what was going on and made a whiny fuss. "What the hell is this?! You made your customers wait for nothing!"

Shinichi didn't bother countering him—that they'd hardly be called customers, since they weren't paying a single dime.

A group of men in peculiar little clothes had been waiting patiently in the distance, but when they heard the squabble, they swarmed around the rabble-rouser.

"Thou must not incite chaos on these grounds. I bid thee leave!"

"Hyah!"

""""Who the hell do you—agh!""""

The men didn't hesitate to throw a few punches to his gut, silencing him, before dragging him away.

Shinichi followed with his eyes before calling out the to leader of the group, a round and portly young man. "Captain, thanks for your help again today."

"Ah, m'lord Shinichi. I would not be a true fan if I did not help dispose of the rubbish," he announced, proudly displaying his strange clothing—a Japanese *happi* coat and headband. "It shames me to see such impropriety from a citizen of this city."

"Ha-ha, you're something else, Captain." Shinichi laughed as he thanked the captain.

He didn't know if it was some quirk of the translation spell, but his speech was translated a bit like some Shakespearean sonnet.

"Well I hope you enjoy yourself!"

"Most certainly, with utmost vigor!"

They flashed each other a thumbs-up, and Shinichi left the group of boys in charge of organizing the onlookers as he went back behind the wooden stage. A hired minstrel was tuning his lute.

"All ready?" Shinichi asked.

"Ready whenever you are," he replied with a quick test strum across the strings of his lute.

Shinichi smiled in response before walking back to the side of the stage to give the maid her instructions.

"Celes, let's go."

"Understood. *Darkness*."

Celes's spell coated the entire area, deepening the already dim shadows cast by the city walls.

"They're gonna start! They're gonna start!"

The crowd started to buzz with excitement as the sound of the lute began to flow gently through the air. At first, the soft notes trickled in, like a gentle breeze, but they suddenly blazed with energy, blasting through the darkness as a rainbow-colored *Light* spell lit the stage and revealed a silhouette standing in the very center.

Her glossy black hair was pulled into adorable little pigtails on either side of her head. She wore a short plaid skirt and vest, designed by Shinichi, weaved by one of the Arachne spider ladies. Her fluttering clothes captivated the audience, filling their eyes with this rare, other-worldly design.

Her slender legs were covered by knee-high socks. Her bare leg peeked out from time to time. These were rare moments that the audience savored.

She was seriously a perfect angel who'd descended onto the mining town, and her name was—

""""RINOOO!""""

"Let's go, everybodyyy!"

Amplified by magic, her voice echoed and pierced through the deep, hoarse cheers of adult men. Following the beat, cutesy teddy bears and rabbit plushies walked up on stage and started dancing along with Rino.

"I jumped under the red sun, from the world with the blue sun, where I first saw the blue sky. ♪"

Her singing voice mixed with the upbeat sounds of the lute.

It was completely different from the usual heroic sagas of the minstrels and the holy hymns on the Goddess's love. This was pop music. It was about a girl's fears and love after coming to a new world—you know, cliché, relatable, resonating with all who listen.

"In that sky, which spreads so far, swallowed by moon and stars, do you know what my heart is trying to say? ♪"

Rino leaped into the air, her skirt fluttering, and the dolls tried their very best to move their tiny legs and feet and jump in the exact same way.

They were golems. Celes had made them based on Shinichi's sketches and *Linked* them to Rino's movements. But the children in the audience didn't know that. They wholeheartedly believed them to be real animals.

"Ahh, Rino, you're so cute!" The kids waved their hands wildly in her direction.

She smiled and waved back. Their parents and grandparents smiled at the exchange and—

""""Oooooh! Rino! Rino! Rino!"""" belted a few deep voices.

With their chubby captain on the front lines, the group of men began to chant without shame.

"Wh-what's this…?"

"An evil ritual?!"

On the sidelines, the holy warriors looked on at the commotion with trepidation, but the cheering men didn't pay them any mind.

"Tell me, what's the color of the sky you see? ♪"

""""Hey, hey, hey!"""" They pumped their fists in the air in perfect unison.

Even without their glow sticks, they were definitely idol devotees.

"Disgusting pedophiles," Celes spat.

"Celes, these stalwart men would treat that as a compliment," replied Shinichi.

She continued to glare from the stage wing, but they didn't take notice and continued to send Rino their fevered chants.

"I want to see it with you someday. ♪"

""""Yeaaaaaah!!"""" As the song came to a close, they released their biggest cheer yet.

Rino smiled in thanks and waved, her little dolls joining her. They didn't have much time for her to memorize songs and accompanying dances, which meant the live show was over after one song, but this was where the real battle began.

"We will now begin selling merch!" Shinichi called out to the pumped-up crowd. "We have these commemorative Rino fans today!" From under the table, he pulled out a bunch of paper fans with her smiling face printed on them.

To make these, the Demon King had first used his *Thoughtography* to burn her smile onto paper. Then, they recruited the demons who were particularly crafty, like the kobolds, to paste them onto the fan frame. He'd made the paper and frames from trees in Dog Valley and a starch-based glue from some potatoes using *Element Conversion*. That meant the grand total of the materials was close to zero, but—

"We're selling 'em at a low, low price of only three silver coins per fan!"

This was around thirty thousand yen—and a complete rip-off. But this was a world without photographs or color copiers. Not to mention, very few magic users were able to cast *Thoughtography*. A portrait could cost upward of a silver piece (around ten thousand yen). He wasn't being dishonest when he said it was a low, low price.

On top of that, this merchandise couldn't be bought in any stores, so real supporters would do anything to get these.

"Yes! Yes! Indeed! I shall buy them!"

"Give me five! Here take these! Fifteen silver pieces!"

With great composure, Shinichi held back the throngs of fanboys. "Okay, please calm down. Supplies are limited, so they will be limited to one per person."

"Members of the Fan Club wearing *happi* coats will have priority. Nonmembers, please line up here," Arian shouted, disguised with glasses and a cap, as she guided the customers like a seasoned pro.

"We just restocked more *happi* coats and headbands as proof of membership! One set costs three large silver pieces, but we only have five, so hurry while they last!" he cried.

He hadn't forgotten that a limited supply really makes people want to buy in a crazed frenzy. There were even non–Fan Club members— people who weren't necessarily trapped in his dirty scheme—who lined up to buy a fan.

"Mama, I want a Rino fan, too!"

"Maybe we should buy one to thank her for healing Grandma's knee."

"I wouldn't be much of a man if I left without showing her my gratitude for resurrectin' me. Hey, I'll take one of those *happi* coat things!"

"No, I have no interest in little girls! But those *happi* coats are just really strange! Yeah, that's definitely all I'm interested in!"

With a few flimsy excuses here and there, the crowd justified their purchases, and the merchandise completely sold out in the blink of an eye.

"Just when I thought they were treating people for free, they put all that effort into this performance, and make money this way...," said one of the holy warriors. He was impressed by the clever sales tactic in spite of himself.

But the Dirty Advisor's final act was yet to come.

"We've sold out of Rino fans. Thank you, everyone! ...Now we'll move to the main item of the day," Shinichi announced.

Celes inched forward very slowly, balancing a silver platter. On it, there was an item covered in a red cloth. Once enough people were looking at the gleaming plate in curiosity, he whipped off the cloth to reveal—

"A one-eighth-scale Rino figurine! Cat-eared version!"

""""Whoooaaa!"""" The fanboys roared an even louder cheer at the sight of the exquisitely crafted clay Rino statuette.

"Cute cat ears and tail? To make an already adorable girl even cuter? A divine idea!"

"I think it's rumored that the demons look like this! But how can it be so lovable?!"

"What doth lie beneath thy skirt?!"

"Buy it and find out." Shinichi placated the frenzied crowd as he signaled for the sale to begin. "We will start at five large silver pieces!"

There was one and only one figurine. The person who bid the highest price would take it home—auction-style. The price started at five large silver pieces (approximately fifty thousand Japanese yen). The average person wouldn't join in to bid so high on a doll.

But the boys wearing their three-large-silver-coins-apiece *happi* couldn't be tamed.

"Eight large silver pieces!"

"One gold piece!"

"Then I bid two gold pieces!"

Each time someone raised their hand, the price would skyrocket.

"Ha-ha-ha, I can't stop laughing! Oh, the manufacturing overhead was just the cost of the clay," Shinichi chuckled.

"You are sick," Celes fumed, but the auction continued to heat up.

"Twenty gold, what sayeth you to that!"

"Is that all you've got? Twenty-five gold coins!"

My daughter's statue is mine! Bring me all the gold bars in the royal coffers! boomed a voice in Shinichi's head.

"Your Highness, please shut up," he telepathized back.

The Demon King had been watching the live show using magic, but Shinichi brushed off his messages.

"Hold thyself still, fifty gold pieces!" shouted the captain, an equivalent to five million yen.

The other members of the group hung their heads begrudgingly.

"This limited edition cat-eared Rino figurine will go to the captain for fifty gold pieces!"

"Ha-ha! Victory!" roared the captain, thrusting his fists in the air with his chubby *happi*-clad silhouette.

The rest of the crowd gave a round of applause, no hard feelings.

The normal customers and holy warriors looked incredulously at the unimaginable idiot. They shot him an icy glare.

But it was easily worth fifty gold pieces. After all, it was sculpted expertly by the dwarves, the masters of forge and craft, and it was a one-of-a-kind piece of fine art.

"Okay, Rino," Shinichi said. "Would you please hand the captain his prize?"

"Yessiree!" she replied, running out from where she'd been taking a short break. She blushed at the figure of herself as she held it. "I'm very happy that you purchased it, but I'd hate for you to look at it too much. It'd make me embarrassed, you know?"

"Fear not, I shall only view it twenty hours a day!" boasted the captain.

Isn't that pretty much all day? the crowd wanted to interject, but Rino placed it in his hands with a smile.

"I didn't realize you liked dolls. I do, too. It makes me happy to make friends who have the same hobby."

"Indeed, we are much alike!"

Yeah, your interest in dolls is realllllllyy not the same as hers. Of course, no one voiced this concern, either.

The captain accepted the figurine from Rino, gently squeezing her hand to shake it.

"Gah, I'm so jealous…!" The group gritted their teeth.

"Ha-ha-ha, these are the spoils of victory!" boasted the captain with a jiggle of his pudgy stomach.

Shinichi smiled as he watched them, until he made another announcement—

"Next, we have another Rino figurine, bunny girl version," he crooned, throwing fuel onto the fire.

"This one has soft, fluffy bunny ears! And what's with this scandalous outfit?!"

"Criminal! Illegal! I'll take it for ten gold pieces."

"Whooaa, thirty gold pieces!"

"Captain, you won the last one! Don't steal this one, too!"

"Gah, you're a coward for stabbing me in the back!"

"Please stop fighting!" Rino yelled over them, trying to stop the idiots and their red-hot tempers from blazing over.

Shinichi watched the scene but stepped away from the table. "Arian, I leave the rest to you."

"Yeah, you sure?" She wasn't quite certain what he was up to.

Shinichi kept an eye on her as he walked to the shadows of the buildings, making a beeline for the Saint and her holy warriors, who had been watching this entire time.

"Oh-ho, Saint Sanctina, I hope you are well today, m'lady."

"Bastard, you're being too familiar with her!" shouted a holy warrior, vexed by his sarcastic greeting, as he leveled his halberd at Shinichi.

Shinichi didn't flinch back and kept his eyes locked on to the Saint's. Her smile stayed the same.

"And? How can I help you? We're sold out of fans and *happi* coats at the moment," he jeered.

"We've come to ask you to stop offering healing services," she replied.

"What?!" Shinichi yelped theatrically to this completely expected response. "*You?* The kind and gentle Saint? *You're* telling us to put an end to our wonderful charity and stop saving the ill and injured—at no cost?!"

"Hey, keep your voice down!" barked one of her men, trying in a panic to rein him in.

Shinichi had been shouting loud enough to make sure everyone could hear him, even over the hubbub of the show and auction. But he complied with the warrior's demand.

"So you're saying we have to stop doing charity work for the people?" he asked the Saint again.

"Yes, I'm asking you to please stop."

"Why?"

"It goes against the Goddess's teachings," she explained, still smiling. She didn't hesitate for a single moment. "Saving those who suffer, giving life to those decreased, that's our divine mission handed to us by the Goddess Elazonia."

"Yes, it's *our* duty as followers of the Goddess. Others shouldn't meddle in our affairs!" bleated another man.

They packed in closer to him, but Shinichi didn't so much as flinch.

"And yet," he stated, "for whatever reason, you've inflated the required donations by five times and stopped performing resurrections. That forced the people to come to us, right?"

"W-well, that…" The holy warriors recoiled in face of this logical response.

But the smiling Saint didn't waver one bit. "That was unavoidable. The king refused our request."

"Hmm, I have no idea what request that might be. But it seems you're telling the townsmen to either follow the Goddess or eff off and die. What do you have to say for yourself?"

"……" The Saint didn't answer.

By saying *no*, she would have to lie, and that's unacceptable for a saint.

By saying *yes*, she'd be acknowledging that the church oppressed its people, and that's also not acceptable from a saint.

Instead of waiting for her response, one of the holy warriors shouted out, "It's necessary to defeat the sinister beasts in Dog Valley!"

"Is that so? But these demons haven't done anything to Tigris Kingdom, no? Are you seriously asking them to sacrifice their lives to defeat them? The people here have nothing to gain from this. Are you sure you aren't just harassing them?"

"How dare you mock the Goddess's will to destroy these monsters!" bellowed the warrior in anger, bringing his halberd to Shinichi's throat.

But he trudged forward without fear. "I have no issues with the Goddess's teachings, but I think the people of the city are pretty annoyed by how you do things, yeah?"

He turned back to look at the crowd, all their eyes on him. Half of them cast their eyes down as they hurried off, unwilling to get pulled into direct confrontation. But the remaining few were boldly glaring at the holy group with open hostility.

"As you can see, it looks like you have quite a few enemies. What do you think, Saint?" Shinichi asked.

"……"

"Why don't you try to look cute? Why don't you sing and dance a bit? I bet the men in this city would start to like you more if you bounced that huge rack of yours." He smirked.

"You filth!" snarled the warriors, this time ready to stab him.

He took the opportunity to step back and take his leave. In his place, the group of fanboys stepped up to close in on the warriors.

"Doth enthusiasm for Rino's performance spill from even the church disciples? No bother, for overjoyed am I to lay eyes on a kindred spirit!"

"What the hell is with these guys? Get away! Shoo!" warned one of her holy men.

"Say not such cruel words, for today we shall revel in stories of Rino until the sun doth show its face!"

"G-get away, you freaks! Lady Sanctina, I think we should take our leave for today."

"…Yes," she replied.

They may have been good at lecturing the teachings of the Goddess, but they really didn't like being on the receiving end of things. The holy team lost ground to the captain's boys and decided to make a run for it.

Shinichi smiled wryly and went back to the site of the auction, where Arian was starting to clean up.

"Thanks for your help. Sorry I left you with the cleanup, too."

"No problem. What kind of horrible things were you saying to them?" she asked as she looked with pity at the holy warriors.

As they fled the scene, they kept glancing back with unbridled rage in their eyes.

Shinichi let out a chuckle, as if offended by her question.

"You're so mean to me. What do I look like? You think I look like a dirty, twisted dude who'd enjoy messing around with a bunch of hardheaded numbskulls?"

"Well yeah, you're totally sick!" She smiled radiantly.

"…So you've started saying it, too," said Shinichi in some kind of perverted relief as he patted her on her shoulders.

That's when Rino walked up to him, freshly changed out of her show clothes, alongside Celes.

"How is this related to overthrowing the Saint?" asked Celes.

"I don't really understand, either. Like, I'm really happy I can make everyone else happy with music and magic, but…" Rino trailed off.

"I see, then let's walk through the plan again."

As the team stepped out of the city gates, far enough so that none of the residents could overhear their scheme, Shinichi laid out his entire plan.

"Goal number one: Stop the conductor from collecting any more magic," he started.

There weren't many devout followers, meaning that they only went to the cathedral for healing injuries and illnesses. They gave their magic to the conductor because they were coerced into it.

That meant once they heard Rino was doing it for free, they'd have no reason to go to the cathedral.

"The Saint dug her own grave when she stopped their normal operations because of a measly little fight with the king. They should lose more and more people as time goes on."

"Well, we'll become busier and busier," muttered Celes. She didn't want to keep pushing Rino to exhaustion and glared a bit at Shinichi, who raised his hands in apology.

"Goal number two: Improve the relationship between the demons and humans," he continued.

They would provide this free healing alongside entertainment to the people—song and dance. It wouldn't be hard to steal the people's hearts with these performances. After all, they were completely unheard of and new to this world, brought to life through his twenty-first-century knowledge and experience.

"Once she's super-popular, she can reveal that she's a demon, and that'll totally eliminate some of the prejudices and stereotypes."

"I wonder if it would really go that well…," murmured Arian. She wasn't completely on board, especially when she thought back on her painful memories as a half dragon.

"Obviously, it wouldn't go swimmingly with everyone right away. But humans are self-centered. They won't hate someone if they believe that person would benefit them, even if it's a demon," explained Shinichi.

Since the church publicly declared that the demons were their sworn enemies, there wouldn't be many people willing to defend them. But if more and more people started to believe there were good demons like Rino, the humans and demons would eventually be able to make peace.

"They say Rome wasn't built in a day. We have to be patient."

For example, his goal was to make a fun country, but that wasn't something that could happen overnight. That's what made it worth doing.

"Goal number three: Sell merchandise and make money."

Yeah, there was an absurd amount of gold in the Demon King's castle, but it wasn't a bottomless supply. They were putting a lot of it into buying food. That's why he wanted to build the knowledge and expertise necessary to run a successful business.

"Plus, people would start to get suspicious that there's some hidden cost if you tell them you're doing free volunteer work. They actually trust you more if you show them your greedy side."

"It's a twisted way to think, but it does have its own logic," Celes agreed with a sigh. She knew the demon society didn't revolve around good intentions, either.

"And finally, the most important one…goal number four: Get the Saint to see us as an enemy."

"You want her to hate us?" asked Rino skeptically. She thought they were going to try to become friends with her and persuade her to stop fighting the demons.

But this process was a necessary step toward making her like them.

"The Saint showed absolutely no interest in me, even though I saved her life. She probably has no interest in other people. If we stand in her way as an enemy, she'll at least *see* us. We need to take what we can get," he explained.

The opposite of love isn't hate. It's indifference.

As long as they remained several of many faceless people in her life, nothing they said would ever reach her.

Hatred was a negative emotion, but she'd have some interest in something she despised.

"A certain god once said: 'Hate can be transformed into love.'"

You had a strong feeling toward someone you hated. They left an impression on you. Even though it was far more negative than love, this person was important enough that they took up residence in your heart.

"So we can use the effect where a bad guy does something a little good, and they'll see it as really good, since it contrasts their normal behavior so much. That'll change hate to love."

The gap effect showed that if the first event a person witnessed was very bad, you could take advantage of the difference between that and the second event to leave someone with a strong impression. Obviously if you hate a person too much, it doesn't matter what they do, you'll see it as a bad thing.

Well, even if it doesn't go that well, as long as the Saint hates me, I can draw her attention away from the Demon King.

If she hated Shinichi more than the Demon King, then she'd aim to kill him before anyone else, meaning he'd send her on a wild goose chase to protect the castle.

And if it really comes down to it...

Shinichi vocalized the black thoughts swirling in the darkest recesses of his mind. Because of this, the girls started to be suspicious of him.

"Are you going after the Saint again...?" asked Arian nervously with the shifty eyes of an abandoned dog.

"If you like big boobs that much, shouldn't you raise some cows?" Celes asked, glaring icily at him as if he were some pervert.

Rino was the only one who was concerned for his well-being—too young to understand romantic love. "I don't really understand, but I'd be sad if someone hated you…"

"I don't care who hates me, as long I've got you," Shinichi said, hugging her svelte body. He was just happy that she was so pure and so kind.

"Aaaah!" Arian yelped.

"If you have time to sexually harass Lady Rino, you have time to defeat the Saint."

"All right, now that I have Celes's permission, I'll put everything I have into my attack strategy against the Saint!" declared Shinichi, pumping a fist in the air.

"But *I* don't want to give you permission…," whispered Arian from behind him, fear dripping from her voice.

At this point, no one knew whether her fears would come true or not.

There was a time when Sanctina, age five, had sat in the garden of the children's home plucking white petal after white petal from a wildflower. There wasn't anything to do after her lessons on magic and religious teachings. She was counting the petals, trying to tell her fortune, when the slim fingers of her caretaker grasped her wrist to stop her.

"Stop that. This isn't appropriate for a child chosen by the Goddess."

"Yes, ma'am," she obliged, tossing the bare flower to the side.

The woman smiled at the obedient child and led her back to the home by the hand.

But she made the small mistake of not explaining why: that Sanctina shouldn't engage in such behavior and should feel sorry for the flower, for damaging it.

At age twelve, she'd received the goddess's blessing to become a hero and led a group of five holy warriors to exterminate a colossal monster—a magically mutated bear.

"*Ice Javelin.*"

As she chanted her incantation, the water particles in the air glinted and sharped their edges to become spears of ice—piercing through the length of the monster, all thirteen feet, and killing it immediately.

"Incredible, Lady Sanctina," marveled the holy warriors.

As they praised and lauded her, they convulsed in fear, deep in their guts, at the sight of a child less than half their age wielding such incredible spells.

That wasn't anything out of the ordinary.

But that was when a small cub lumbered out from the den behind the lifeless form of the collapsed bear.

"It had a child," one of the holy men remarked. Their faces showed some surprise, but it wasn't that shocking an event.

After all, monsters were normal animals. They'd only taken the forms of beasts by absorbing large quantities of magic. If there were creatures in an area with air that had high magic density, they could transform into these crude forms.

As it turned out, the massive corpse on the ground was once a mama bear. The cub hadn't transformed into a beast but growled aggressively at the humans, his mother's murderers.

"If we let it grow up as it is, it'll hold a grudge against us and attack us in the future," warned the eldest holy warrior as he drew his sword.

He stopped when a new recruit called out to Sanctina: "That cub is a threat to humanity. It's your duty as a hero to eliminate it."

He was trying to harass and bully her. He was jealous of her powers, especially because she was significantly younger than him.

"Hey! Don't make the hero waste time on such tiny—," the older one reprimanded, as he tried to handle it himself, but he was far too slow.

"*Stone Blast.*"

Small pebbles and stones catapulted toward the cub, aiming for its skull and shattering its bones. As the fresh smell of lukewarm blood hung in the air, Sanctina turned to the distressed young warrior with a warm smile.

"Was that good?"

"Y-yeah, as I'd expect from the hero Sanctina!" he squeaked, his face pinched and hands shaking as he applauded.

There was nothing wrong with eliminating a future threat.

But they made a mistake in not telling her it was all right to be sad.

All they did was praise her for taking its life.

When she was thirteen, she was already developing into a woman, her feminine beauty starting to blossom and bloom.

Sanctina had received a gift—a thank-you from a noble family for cutting down a monster in their area. It was a magnificent ball gown and brilliantly red shoes.

When Cronklum returned to the mansion, Sanctina tried them on to show him.

He smiled kindly but warned her, "Such gaudy clothing isn't appropriate for a Saint. Never wear it again."

"Yes, sir," she avowed, immediately scampering off to remove them.

She burned them with her own magic.

As word of her saintliness spread, he became more and more paranoid that others would start to gossip: "Has she finally become more sensual?" "Does she have her eye on a certain boy?" A single rumor could jeopardize her value as a saint.

It's still not certain whether or not his fears were justified.

But he made a big mistake by not praising his adopted daughter who'd glammed up to show him.

If they knew more about her life, most people would feel sympathy for Sanctina—maybe even pity her unhappiness. They'd think, *She had no freedom*, or *She was brainwashed*, or *She's never known the love of a parent*.

But those were arbitrary judgments, projections of their own beliefs.

The fact was, she was satisfied. She'd been a child loved by the Goddess, an undying hero, then a pure and undefiled saint, an existence that she chose for herself.

Far away from the main part of the city, things proceeded as usual: Rino healed the injured, she performed on stage, and then they started to sell her merch.

"We're going with a raffle today," announced Shinichi, dropping a large box on the table. "One ticket is two silver pieces. Prize D is three Rino postcards, Prize C is a Rino mug, Prize B is a mini Rino figurine, and Prize A is…one of Rino's stage outfits!"

""""WHOOO!"""" The men of the Fan Club yelped with excitement, loud enough to shake the ground and be mistaken for an earthquake—as Shinichi held up the small plaid outfit.

"I must win!"

"Wait, Captain, a ticket for that might not even be in there!" warned a voice in the crowd.

It seemed this kind of scam existed in any world.

Shinichi had anticipated as much. A small smile rose to his face as he placated them: "Winning tickets are in there. If you don't believe me…you can pull the lottery until the box is empty."

""""Oh right!"""" all the idiots with too much disposable income shouted in unison, satisfied with the setup.

"I shall purchase fifty tickets for one gold!"

"Ah, the Fan Club will have priority, but it's limited to one ticket per purchase. After you take your ticket, head to the back of the line," Shinichi instructed.

"What?! Agh, if't must be so, t'would be better to wait and pull from the last dregs of tickets when Lady Luck wouldst smile upon me…no, for if the prize were won ahead of me, all hope would be lost…"

"Captain, I'm going first," said one of the men.

"Ha, this guy's lucky! You've drawn the secret prize! A ticket for one handshake with Rino!" Shinichi exclaimed.

"Seriously?! Yeaaah!"

"There's secret prizes?!" shouted the remaining boys in surprise.

"Then I shall purchase as many tickets as possible with great haste, even if I must do so one at a time!"

Shinichi couldn't stop laughing as he watched the fans throw down two silver pieces (two thousand yen) without hesitation, screaming in joy or sorrow at the results.

"Ha-ha-ha, we're raking it in!" he telepathized. *"We spent almost nothing making the prizes, but I bait them with the grand prize, and they just keep comin'!"*

"Please refrain from sending me your sick and twisted telepathic messages." Celes sighed as usual.

Though Shinichi was smiling genially on the surface, he cackled evilly on the inside.

"I must say, His Highness would be very angry if he found out you were selling Lady Rino's used clothing to these perverted pigs. What do you have to say for yourself?"

"Celes, I never once said that Rino's so-called 'stage outfit' had been used!"

"Oh, that's twisted."

She was thinking that it was a bit of a scam, but the fanboys were so delirious with excitement that they'd probably put a new outfit on their altars and worship it anyway.

Fortunately, a father and his little girl won the outfit. No one could be angry that she won, seeing that she cried in joy at being able to dress just like Rino.

"I didn't even rig it...seems there really is a god in this world," Shinichi remarked, impressed by the way things turned out.

"God has abandoned meeeeee!" sobbed the captain, who'd bought three tickets, each of them Prize D.

After Shinichi watched the rest of the boys take him away, he glanced over to the shadows of the buildings a little ways off. "She's here again."

Sanctina was covered in a robe, a poor excuse for a disguise, as she stared in their direction. Shinichi had expected her to do more to hinder their activities, but she was held back by the Fan Club and city people milling about. She just stood there, peeking out at them.

"Are you going to go heckle her again?" asked Arian, a little concerned, but Shinichi shook his head.

"Nah, not today. If I push her too hard, it'll have the opposite effect. Sometimes pulling away makes them notice you more."

"…Shinichi, you seem really experienced with this kind of thing," noted Arian in a voiced tinged with jealousy, but he just laughed at his own expense.

"Everything I know, I got from books and the Internet. I haven't learned this from actual experience, so I don't have a clue whether it'll work or not."

"Really?"

"Yep. You're the first girl I've ever tried to flirt with."

"I'm the first…hee-hee." Arian giggled, her face flushing deep red, melting into a puddle of a smile.

Shinichi blushed a little, too.

"Did you learn how to do that from the books, too?" Celes telepathized.

"Heeeey, Rino, time to go soon," called Shinichi as she chatted with the minstrel.

"Okay!"

"All right, see you tomorrow."

The minstrel waved with one hand, the lute in his other as he walked away.

"What did he say to you?" asked Shinichi.

"Oh, he said it's not enough to have just one song. He'd like to make more."

"Ah, yeah, I was thinking the same thing…," he admitted, scratching the side of his head in puzzlement as he took the smartphone out of his pocket.

It had already been a month since he'd been summoned into this world, which meant the battery had run completely dry. Thankfully, he'd kept his charger on him, and he'd been casting a *Lightning* spell on the plug to charge it. He was able to have Rino and the minstrel listen to the music on it. That's how they were able to do these live performances in the first place, but—

"I'm worried it's going to break any moment…"

He'd cast the spell with a hundred volts in mind, matching the electrical outlets in Japan, but he had no idea if he'd done it properly. He wouldn't be too surprised if someday it just broke in his hands, fried.

Even though Shinichi didn't get attached to material things, this smartphone was one of the few pieces of proof that he'd ever existed on Earth. He was reluctant to break it.

"Well, this is what it's for anyway. All right, once we get home, we'll have some special singing lessons and dance practice to make a new song!"

"I'll do my best!" exclaimed Rino, bouncing up and down as Shinichi led them out of the city.

From the shadows of the buildings, the Saint's eyes followed them as they got farther away.

After Celes teleported them back to the Demon King's castle, the group had some dinner and rested a little bit before gathering in Rino's room to start practicing the new song.

"All right, you'll need to memorize this," Shinichi explained.

"Yep!" Rino yelled.

"Understood," said Celes.

Shinichi took out the phone and opened up an app. Rino and Celes were sitting on either side of him, watching intently. The app was a music video game, one that a geeky friend of his kept insisting he try. It let you play as an idol.

"I never imagined the day when this would be useful in another world...," he muttered, feeling some complicated feelings as he fired up the game.

It was a pretty normal music game. You had to tap on beat whenever a circle flashed on the center of the screen. But the most important part was the 3-D characters that danced and sang on the screen.

If all they needed was music, he had a ton of songs saved on this phone. But this game was perfect for memorizing dances.

"Would have been even better if I'd saved videos of idols performing live," Shinichi lamented.

"Wow, Miss Orange is so cute!" Rino was glued to the screen as Shinichi played the game, not missing a single beat even though he was lost in thought.

"All right, that's it. You two got it all?"

"Completely!" said Rino.

"Absolutely no issues," confirmed Celes.

The two girls nodded emphatically as he turned off the phone, afraid of letting the battery run out.

"Even if we forget, we can use *Search* magic to remember," the maid remarked.

"That spell's a bit like cheating, huh?"

"You're the person who created it. Are you seriously the one to talk?" Celes's annoyed expression was mixed with just a little approval.

Shinichi smiled wryly. "I know you couldn't come up with *Search* 'cause you've got no idea how the brain or memory works. But I bet you could've imagined and made something like *Perfect Memory*."

"Maybe. It would take time to solidify the image in my mind but should be possible."

The average magic user would be petrified to hear Celes say that so offhandedly. It's easy to explain the workings of a magic spell in theory: It's a way to change reality to match your imagination. But it was more difficult in practice: to clearly envision what you want.

For example, if you told someone to imagine themselves flying through the sky, a person in modern Japan would have no problem, since they were familiar with out-of-this-world inventions in anime and movies.

But the average person in this other world of Obum would have doubts sneaking into the back of their mind, like *Humans don't have wings, so there's no way they could fly.* That kind of hesitation would make a *Fly* spell fail.

It mattered less how much magic power someone had and more if they could see it in their mind's eye. Otherwise, they wouldn't be able to cast the spell. However, Celes had a great imagination, giving her the ability to change the world to match her desired image with ease.

On the flip side, her imagination is so strong that she tends to look down on other people...

Shinichi turned to Celes with a wry smile, at which she hid her voluptuous chest under her hands, expressionless as always.

"Stop fantasizing about putting me in flashy clothing and humiliating me," she sneered.

"I wasn't! But if I want to fantasize, I will!" yelled Shinichi, giving her a piece of his mind.

She just gave him her normal scornful glare before turning and bowing slightly to Rino. "Well then, I'll begin writing the lyrics."

"Thank you!" cheered Rino with an encouraging smile as Celes left the room.

If Rino sang the original Japanese lyrics, they wouldn't make sense to anyone.

On the other hand, if they used *Translation*, it could technically translate words like *bibiana* to "roast," but it would be stilted and the increase in syllables would mess up the tempo. Even if it that wasn't the case, the lyrics were tailored to a modern Japanese audience. Phrases like *I met you on the train on my way to work* didn't mean anything to these people.

This meant they needed to rewrite the lyrics from scratch. Celes was perfect for the job, as she excelled in imagination and language skills.

"When I let Arian take a stab at it, everything she wrote was so sickly sweet..." He winced, eyes growing distant.

"I-I thought it was cute and nice," offered Rino, desperately trying smooth things over, but the lilt in her voice made her sound like she was uncertain and unconvinced by her own words.

"Well anyway, we'll put the song aside for now. Let's do some dance practice."

"Okay!"

As Shinichi clapped the beat, Rino used a *Search* spell to recall the images from the game and started dancing slowly.

There wasn't any way for her to conjure a spell to make her body dance in accordance with the memory, meaning she had to go about it the old-fashioned way, practicing until it was muscle memory. But she enjoyed the process, so it was fine.

"One, two, three, yessiree!"

She spun and jumped on rhythm, over and over again, until beads of sweat started to appear on her forehead. Even then, she erupted into a blissful smile.

She'd never really exerted effort before, especially when learning something new. All her life, the Demon King, Celes, and the other demons were always doing things for her. She savored this new experience.

As he watched her enjoying herself, Shinichi wanted to let Rino dance and dance forever, but after about an hour, she started to pant, and they stopped entirely.

"All right, that's all for today."

"Huff, huff… We're done already?" she asked.

"You still need energy to heal the patients and do the performance tomorrow. You shouldn't push yourself too hard," he reminded with a soft smile as he draped a towel over her face. She looked at him, still eager to continue. "Hey, take a bath. Go wash off your sweat. Go to bed for the night."

"…Okay," she agreed sulkily, nodding with much disappointment.

She went to leave the room, but stopped and pulled on his sleeve. "Right! Shinichi, join me!"

"…Huh?"

"Can't you?" She looked up at him with moist eyes, begging him.

He almost nodded yes without thinking. But instead, he shook his head so violently he could have broken his neck. "No, no, no, definitely can't do that!"

"Why not?"

"Well, because you're a girl and I'm a boy, remember?"

"But I take baths with Daddy all the time…"

"Yeah, but he's your *dad*…," he explained, but she didn't seem to understand.

She didn't display a single shred of bashfulness.

Shinichi pondered: *She looks like she's not a day over ten. But I think I heard she's actually fourteen.*

Since the demons lived twice as long as humans, they matured more slowly.

But for her to have no shame or knowledge about the differences between boys and girls? It must be the Demon King's fault for not teaching her…

Based on Celes's reaction, sexual behaviors were taboo for demonkind, too.

The only reason Rino didn't shy away from this topic was because the Demon King had sheltered her and never taught her the birds and the bees. On top of that, she hadn't had much contact with boys her age. She must have grown up without knowing she should be embarrassed about certain things.

I really need to do something about this…

His secret goal for this entire idol scheme was to get Rino to meet children that didn't know she was the daughter of the almighty Demon King. That hadn't ended up panning out, seeing that the crowd comprised patients and fans. Any relationship she could make with them still had a power imbalance and fell pretty short of a mutual friendship.

I'll have to explain something to the King so we can get some non-perverted kids in the castle…and do what exactly? Start an elementary school? I've never seen a demon studying. When we open trade with the humans, they'll need to be able to do basic addition and subtraction…

Shinichi had made a mistake by becoming lost in his thoughts.

When he finally came to, he realized Rino had taken his hand and led him all the way to the dressing room next to the community bath.

"Come on, Shinichi. Hurry up and get undressed," she prompted.

"Huh?! Okay, okay, I can do it myself," he yelped.

At some point, Rino had taken off her clothes. She was now wrapped in a towel as she pulled at his clothes. Shinichi finally gave up and yanked them off, wrapping a towel around his waist and opening the door to the bathroom. In it was a massive stone tub filled to the brim with warm water.

"Good, no one's here," he confirmed, relieved that there was no sight of anyone else in the community bath.

It seemed baths weren't customary for demonkind, who favored quick rinses or using a *Purification* spell to remove dirt and grime from their bodies.

This bath was Shinichi's idea: He'd asked the Demon King for a huge favor when he just couldn't take it anymore. After all, he was Japanese—he loved his baths.

The Wampus cat people and a few other demon species hated water and gave the bath a hard pass. But the majority were so fond of it that there was now a massive community bath on the first floor.

This smaller one was just for Shinichi and his friends.

I'd be dead if Arian or Celes saw us, much less the King... He broke into a cold sweat just thinking about it.

Rino was completely oblivious to this as she climbed into the bath, settling into the warm water and sighing contentedly. "Ahh, I feel alive again."

"Ha-ha, you sound just like an old man," joked Shinichi, chuckling a little, as he slid in next to Rino.

Shinichi might have been a die-hard pervert, but he had enough sense to have some reservations about getting in a bath with a girl, especially a child.

But he did realize one thing: *Rino's really tired, and if she happened to...*

The bathtub was large enough to fit the Demon King, after all, which meant that if she fell asleep, there was a chance that she could end up drowning.

Obviously, he knew she'd probably wake up right away or she could be resurrected, but he couldn't exactly overlook the possibility of a child drowning.

Rino was blissfully unaware of the thoughts racing through his head as she smiled and smiled. "It's been a long time since I've taken a breather with you."

"Is that right?"

"Yep. Lately, we've been busy—me singing songs, you selling things. Before that, you were gone getting food."

"Yeah, I suppose…"

Thinking back, Shinichi *had* been busy, running around, taking care of one thing or another ever since he'd been summoned to this world. There weren't many chances for him to relax and let loose.

The only other time he and Rino had spent time together, just the two of them, was probably when they'd played cat's cradle.

"I know you work hard for us, and I'm very thankful, but sometimes, I want to just talk to you… Is that bad?"

She looked up at him almost apologetically, but Shinichi smiled and stroked her wet hair.

"Of course not. Rino, you're still a kid. You can be a little bit more selfish," he reassured.

Rino looked at him with a pained expression, too mature for her age.

"Thank you, but…we're fighting with the humans because I was selfish and said I wanted to eat yummy food."

"……" Shinichi was lost for words.

"That's why I want to work hard at healing people and singing songs! It's so that we can get along better with the humans!" she continued, balling her fists. It seemed that was her main source of motivation.

After all, the demons advancing into the human world, the ensuing battle between demonkind and humankind, this never-ending

war with the undying heroes under the Goddess's divine protection—all this was her own doing. Even if she hadn't meant for anything bad to happen, she was dealing with the guilt of triggering these events.

Up until now, Shinichi and Celes had been working through the problems with Rino on the sidelines. Being an idol was her first major contribution. That's why Rino worked herself to exhaustion without a single complaint.

"...Rino, you're amazing," he marveled.

He didn't bother to make an awkward attempt at consoling her. He just said what came to mind and tousled her hair again.

"Ah-ha-ha, that tickles." She giggled, but her eyes crinkled in happiness. "By the way, can I ask a question?"

"Sure."

"What kind of place did you used to live in? This *Earth, Japan*?"

"Oh yeah, I guess I haven't told you much about it."

"Yeah, like that *smartphone* thing that makes music! Are there even more amazing things?" Rino asked, her eyes sparkling.

Shinichi thought a moment. "To put it simply, it's a place that's developed thanks to science, instead of magic."

"Science?"

The human world of Obum aside, the demons never made any scientific discoveries beyond a rudimentary level. It just wasn't necessary; they had the convenience of using magic as they pleased. Their level of scientific advancements was on par with ancient times on Earth.

Rino was puzzled by the explanation, cocking her head to the side.

"Yeah, science. It lets us do all sorts of things, like talk to people very far away, fly through the sky in airplanes, blast through the atmosphere to get to outer space."

"How is that different from magic?"

"Ouch, harsh," he joked with a wry smile.

He remembered the famous quote: "Any sufficiently advanced technology is indistinguishable from magic."

"Yeah, I guess it really isn't that different from magic. We could make miracles happen with enough scientific progress, just like magic."

They could change the molecular structure of pebbles to make them gold or use quantum mechanics to teleport people—*or even resurrect the dead*.

"Science, huh…?"

Shinichi loved science, which was why he'd studied the subject so hard.

He had far more knowledge of it than the average high school student, though that wasn't the case for English and his other subjects.

But he had never wanted to become a scientist. Well, more accurately, he did once, but he'd given up on it. It wasn't because he doubted he had the intelligence necessary to become one.

He had a dream that he thought he could achieve as a scientist. But his studies showed him time and time again that it was impossible. Even if science took a step into the realms of magic one day—even a god wouldn't be able to bring back the cremated body of a drowned child, many years ago. It would be impossible to bring a child back to life from memories in brain cells.

"……"

"Shinichi?"

"Ah, sorry, it's nothing," He was pulled out of his thoughts by the sound of her voice. "Well, it was a good world. You could eat all sorts of amazing food there, thanks to science. It's kinda like magic."

He wasn't going to tell her that if you left Japan, blessed in natural resources, there were huge regions far more wretched than even in this world. It would destroy her dreams.

"There's lots of yummy food?!"

"Yeah, there's ice cream, parfaits, curry rice, omurice, just to name a few."

"Woooow, even the names sound delicious!" cried Rino, drooling a little from the corners of her gaping mouth.

Shinichi chuckled as he explained how they were made.

As the conversation meandered on, Rino started to gently nod off. "Parfait...chocolate, I want to...try..."

"I'll carry you back to your room. You go ahead and sleep," he whispered gently.

"...Okay...thank...you..." Her eyes melted shut, and her breaths slowed down.

Shinichi lifted her small body out of the bathtub, stroking his chin as he weighed his options. "Now, how do I dry her off without seeing her naked?"

"Perhaps if I ripped out your eyeballs?"

"That's a good idea—not! ...Huh, what?" he yelped, reflexively shooting back a retort, even as he was frozen in place at the sight of the tanned arm stretching past him.

When he turned around, he saw Celes wrapped in a damp towel and kneeling next to Rino.

"Uh, um, Celes, you're supposed to be writing lyrics, right? When'd you get here?"

"I heard Lady Rino invite you to take a bath, so I went ahead under an *Invisibility* spell."

"Why?!"

"Obviously, to monitor and ensure you didn't attack her with your beastly desires."

"If you're gonna do that, just stop me from going in the first place!" Shinichi snapped.

He wouldn't have had to join Rino if he knew Celes was watching out for her!

But Celes didn't respond as she gently lifted up the sleeping girl. "No one will hear of this from me. Don't worry."

"...So that candy from the Tigris Kingdom... Would one large silver worth of it be enough?"

"I said nothing about requiring a bribe to stay quiet."

"No bribe?"

"Well, if you're offering one gold piece worth of candy, I'd accept." She asked for ten times more.

"Gack…!" Shinichi ground his teeth in frustration, wondering if he'd brought this upon himself.

Celes went to leave the room, cutting off their argument, but stopped before the door closed behind her, remembering something. "By the way, that was the first time I've revealed myself to a man."

"Wait…"

"I presume you'll make an honest woman of me?"

The corners of her mouth pulled up in a pretty little smirk, just like the familiar dirty smile of a certain person, before she softly closed the door.

Shinichi listened until he no longer heard the rustling of clothes. Then he checked to see that they'd left the dressing room.

He returned to the tepid waters, diving underneath so no one could hear him as he screamed. "Stop being a tease!"

He had no idea how much of it was true or how much of it was a joke.

Shinichi began to think no matter how many scientific answers were churned out, even if science could reach and illuminate the darkest recesses of the universe, a man would never, ever be able to understand the confines of a woman's heart.

Saint Sanctina observed from the shadows of the buildings again. The black-haired girl was healing the people of Tigris and working even harder to entertain them.

"Today, I'm going to sing a new song called 'Please! Escalation!' I hope you like it!"

"WHOOOOOO!!" roared the audience.

The crowd easily reached the hundreds, gathering around to watch as

Rino and the adorable puppets began an energetic song and whipped out their dance moves.

"Disgusting fanatics! Working themselves into a frenzy over some evil ritual, idolatry," spat one of Sanctina's men.

"Yeah, but that Rino girl is supercute."

"What did you just say?!"

"I-I'm very sorry."

Sanctina didn't bother listening to the argument between her guards.

The only thing she heard was the girl's song. The only thing she saw was her adorable figure.

But the emotions that stirred and swirled in her heart were something dark, black, like ink—the opposite of the bright stage.

"Our peeping Tom. Ogling young girls on the daily is a hobby that suits you," sneered the black-haired boy, appearing once again.

"Bastard, show some respect!" snarled a holy warrior.

But this verbal abuse didn't reach Sanctina's ears. Instead, she turned her ear toward the words of a child and her grandmother passing by beyond them.

"Grandma, I'm so happy your knee doesn't hurt anymore."

"Me too. Little miss Rino is like our saint."

Saint.

Those words finally made her realize what she was feeling toward that girl—that *Rino.*

"Everyone, let us depart."

"Hey, tucking your tail between your legs and scampering off?" He tried to provoke her, but Sanctina kept her gaze straight ahead as she walked away.

Once they'd made it back to the cathedral, she called all thirty of her holy warriors into the prayer room.

With her back turned to the massive statue of the Goddess, Sanctina spoke with a majestic smile. "Let us destroy that little girl, Rino."

"Huh?!"

"Not the girl! We should be targeting that boy—," objected one of the men, but those words flowed in one ear and out the other.

There was only one thought inside her heart. *Being the Saint,* that *belongs to me.*

She was special, someone others looked up to and worshipped.

She was someone who looked down on humanity from an exalted position—just like the Goddess Elazonia.

She was the one who wasn't allowed to play with flowers, the one who could easily slaughter an abandoned cub, the one who couldn't even dress up like a normal girl. Even then, she was worth something. That's why she did these things.

But Rino was trying to steal that from her.

Sanctina had gone her entire life without showing interest in anything other than being special.

But now, for the first time, she was feeling an emotion toward this usurper of her title.

Those black flames that seared through her entire body were the flames—of hatred.

"They got us good again…"

Shinichi had been joined by his crew as they all lugged boxes full of merch into Tigris Kingdom. But they were all shocked by the sight that greeted them.

Their wooden performance stage and the small wardrobe hut had been completely torn apart. And in the bright blood of a goat or some other animal, the vandals left a threatening message: *Leave, damned outcasts.*

"Who would do—?!" started Arian.

"I don't even need to guess who it was," replied Shinichi, surveying the area and calming her down as she balled her fists, bursting with rage.

Among the people loitering around the fallen stage and gaping in shock, there was one man who looked in their direction with a bold smile. He turned his back to them.

Shinichi used *Search* to look into his own mind. Sure, the man's clothes had been changed, and he was disguised as a commoner, but his face was the same as one of Sanctina's holy warriors.

"I'll go beat him down," Celes declared.

"Hang on. No need for that. This is actually good for us," assured Shinichi as he grabbed her just before she chased after the hated man with the intention to kill.

It was just about that moment when a particular voice rang out from among the crowd.

"What hath befallen the stage?!"

It was the familiar *happi*-clad headband-wearing pudgy figure, the captain of the Fan Club boys. He looked at the destroyed stage and hustled toward Shinichi in a panic.

"Sir Shinichi, this must be no other..."

"Than the people from the church. Yeah, that's obvious," finished Shinichi.

They asked the group of people gathered, but there had been no witnesses. But it all came down to the same suspect.

"Those bastards think Rino stole their customers. That's why they did this despicable thing!"

"It's their fault anyway, isn't it? They're the ones who raised the cost of healing and stopped doing resurrections, right?"

"I don't care if this is to defeat the demons or whatever. They just do whatever they like without thinking about how it affects us...!"

Tensions were growing at the scene, as one grievance piled upon another, but a young hardworking voice cut through it all.

"Everybody, please don't be mad! I'll do my best to heal and sing even without a stage!"

"Rino..."

She should have been the one most upset by the destruction of the stage, but instead, she was brave. The enraged crowd couldn't keep the smiles from returning to their faces.

"That's right! You can sing anywhere you want," encouraged the minstrel, joining them without anyone noticing.

"Leave the stage to us. We'll have it fixed right as rain by tomorrow," offered some miners, flexing their muscles as they threw in their contribution.

"Of course! We shall become the stage!" cried the captain.

"Oh right!" cried the perverts from the Fan Club as they all dropped to their hands and knees left and right.

"Now, Lady Rino, you may climb atop us and sing!"

"Um, but then I'll hurt all of you…"

"I would pay to be walked on by a damsel as lovely as yourself!"

The herd of pigs was red-eyed, hoping for a glance under her skirt.

The maid glared coldly enough to freeze them all, and she spoke a one-word incantation. *"Wind."*

"Oink!"

"Now that the trash has been removed, shall we begin healing the patients?"

"Y-yes, please."

With indignation in their eyes, the fanboys glanced around at the crowd for sympathy, any sympathy at all, but none of the people who met their gazes responded to their voiceless pleas.

"Hmph, I must say I have never had the pleasure of being treated so inappropriately by a maid. A fresh new experience."

"You don't learn, do you?" Shinichi chuckled dryly as he offered a hand to the captain.

The fanboy wasn't angry. If anything, he looked pretty pleased.

The captain accepted the hand and stood, whispering in a low voice. "Sir Shinichi, I find it most unlikely that the church would kindly retreat after this."

"You think so, too?"

"I do. They are more vengeful than a serpent, more spiteful than a wicked stepmother."

"I can see that."

They were talking about the religion that gave birth to the heroes—beings who relentlessly continued pursuing their target, resurrecting even when they died. When it came down to the followers of the religion and the Goddess herself, they were bound to be more persistent. He could apprize as much.

"Say, Captain, you seem to really dislike the church."

"'Tis that how I appear to thee?"

"I mean, yeah, you kept following around and chasing off the holy warriors whenever they tried to stop the healings or the performances. You didn't know if they'd punch you now or exact revenge later."

It could've been explained by the fact that the captain was a diehard Rino fan, but Shinichi had sensed something more personal underlying his motive. It seemed like the captain wanted to harass and provoke the church.

Shinichi confessed he had no proof, just his gut feeling.

The captain smiled dryly and nodded, impressed by his perceptiveness. "Thou art most observant. However, mine is an unfounded resentment."

"Meaning?"

"My father was beset by an incurable malady and passed from this world."

A priest had told them that this disease was incurable—just like old age—refusing to do anything more than cast some magic to relieve his pain.

"With some connections and pulled strings, a healer cast some magic on him. But alas, his condition worsened."

"An illness that gets worse with healing, huh…?"

"And so my esteemed father passed before his time, having lived a mere fifty years. He jested that 'twas his fate, but this foolish son of his would have liked him to stay longer." The captain chuckled, joking that he could have taken it easy if his father were still alive.

But he couldn't hide the loneliness in his eyes.

"So that's why you resent them, huh, even though they've done nothing wrong?"

It isn't like the captain to be this sad, Shinchi worried. *He might be a pervert, but he's usually so bright and cheerful, carefree.*

The captain rubbed his protruding belly, his voice dropping to an even quieter whisper. "'Twould be another story were I to believe it truly was incurable..."

"So you think they could have healed it but didn't?"

Shinichi flashed him an incredulous look, asking whether there was any proof.

The captain nodded deeply. "The malady that beset my father is most commonplace. As one ages, 'tis more common, such that more than half of those who have reached their seventies have experienced it."

That's why it was said that their life was divinely willed to come to a close, and the church didn't offer to resurrect those who died from his disease.

"However, I have not once heard tell of the pope or cardinals suffering from such a malady."

The current pope was pushing ninety. His life was coming to an end, but there was no talk that he was suffering from any illness. On top of that, the four cardinals ranged in age from their fifties to their sixties, but none of them had become acquainted with illness. They were lively and energetic, fighting for the long-term position of pope.

"Even when I unraveled our history, I was unable to find any record of a high-ranking church member passing from such a malady."

If he brought this to their attention, Shinichi could imagine the clergy saying, "Why, of course. We're heroes, and we've received her blessing, after all." But—

"My heart speaks: It has told me they possess the cure," said the captain, chuckling at himself—maybe he was just running from the truth...

that he'd develop this illness at a young age, following in his father's footsteps. Maybe he was just doubting their bogus story because he was afraid to face this fate.

But Shinichi didn't laugh off the captain's fears. He was lost in thought with a very serious look casting over his eyes.

"Captain, where did the illness affect your father?"

"'Twas his stomach. He suffered much pain and lost all desire to eat, slowly wasting away."

"Did he happen to drink a lot or smoke a lot? Or did he eat nothing but meat and avoid all vegetables?"

"'Tis as thou sayeth. He was a great lover of drink and his magnificent belly far did surpass mine."

The captain seemed confused as to how Shinichi had known.

The name of only one disease came to mind: burdening one's body with alcohol and, it went without saying, work-related stress, an illness that was more likely with age.

That was—

"Cancer, maybe?"

Based on his guess, the captain's father died of stomach cancer.

"Cancer?"

"I can't be certain, but if it were cancer, I wouldn't be surprised if healing magic wasn't effective."

When you have cancer, your body makes abnormal cells with damaged DNA. These are different from normal cells, which function in accordance with your DNA, the blueprint of your body. This is why their numbers are under control. For example, if you're injured, normal cells will multiply until they seal the wound. The body won't make more cells than needed.

On the other hand, the cancerous cells don't have a limit, pumping out more and more cells, and multiplying enough to kill the person.

"If he had cancer, it also explains why the healing spells didn't work."

These spells were basically a system to heal bodily abnormalities, injuries, and illnesses, using the patient's DNA as a template.

The problem was when it came to cancer, the spell couldn't distinguish between normal and abnormal DNA, even if someone was clearly ill, since this abnormality was hidden in the person's natural state.

With proper knowledge of cancer, someone could probably remove these cells—or someone with as much power as the Demon King might be able to heal it through brute force, but...

It was easy to see why an average magic user without any knowledge of DNA could make it worse.

Shinichi had fallen into silent contemplation.

The captain looked at him with an expression more serious than Shinichi had ever seen. "Sir Shinichi, is this cancer malady curable?" he asked.

"Ah, yeah. Theoretically, if you remove the bad areas affected by cancer and then use the healing spell, you should be able to heal it."

Of course, there weren't any surgeons, much less those specializing in removing tumors, in a world blessed with healing spells and whatnot. That said, if they just removed the entire area affected by cancer then cast *Full Healing*, only the remaining normal cells would multiply. An effective—albeit somewhat heavy-handed—treatment was fully possible.

Shinichi's explanation was difficult to understand, especially for someone with limited medical knowledge. The captain only understood half of it.

But there was one thing he understood completely.

"...So the church did let him die." He'd forgotten to speak in his usual sonnet form, and his voice frosted over.

It wasn't impossible to think this was the case: The church had their priests dissect the dead to improve their healing spells. And seeing how long their leaders lived, they must have known a way to heal cancer.

But they left the captain's father and other cancer patients out on the streets to die, as long as the chosen people were free of cancer and living long lives. They only thought of themselves.

"...Unforgivable," gritted out the captain, his face contorted in fury.

When he saw Shinichi's surprise, he immediately switched back to his normal jovial self.

"Even so, Sir Shinichi. So young yet in possession of such knowledge. A master of many a field: medicine, entertainment—I have never met or heard of such a genius."

"Well, you'll never guess by my looks that I'm a scholar with more than ten years of studying under my belt."

He was actually just a student.

But in comparison with the people of this world, he could easily get away with calling himself some sort of sage. Anyway, he was instantly regretting the fact that he'd carelessly blabbed on and on about his Earthbound knowledge and needed to find a quick cover-up.

The captain nodded and smiled. "Ah, so you were a teacher. Thy knowledge tempts me to ask for thy tutelage."

"Sorry, I already have a very important student," replied Shinichi and glanced at Rino, who'd just finished her healing spells for the day. She was gearing up to start the performance.

"Aaah, 'twould have passed me by!" he cried as he started to rush off to help with the show, but he stopped and left Shinichi with a few words: "I beg thee be ever vigilant of the church."

"Yeah, I'll be careful."

Shinichi watched the captain run back to the boys of the Fan Club and cry out to Rino. Shinichi then looked at the debris from the destroyed stage and chuckled to himself.

Dear Saint, it seems I've peeved you enough that you can't see how your actions will lose you the people's support and put your goal of defeating the Demon King even further away... Ha-ha, these developments are good for me, though.

It was easier to manipulate someone overcome with anger than someone who could keep their cool.

While Shinichi was gloating about the progress he was making on his strategy, he failed to see one major mistake.

He had become all too familiar and comfortable with Rino's good-ness, wholesomeness. He failed to see there was potential for the Goddess to hate her—more than she hated him for his crude and inso-lent remarks.

The very next day, under the rebuilt stage—thanks to the miners—they finished the performance without a single hitch, flowing directly into their usual merch sale.

"Today we have Rino photographs—thirty images plus a special edition photograph. They are sold in packets of three! Which ones you get are a surprise!"

"Dost thou mean to say we must purchase at least eleven packs for a complete set?!" the captain surmised.

"No, we might get doubles, so we'd have to buy dozens…," lamented another fanboy.

"Underhanded! Devil, demon, Evil God!" cried the captain.

"Well, well, well, if you hate it that much, you don't have to buy it, but…the special edition shows Rino in a wedding dress."

"I shall purchase thirty packs!"

Shinichi was armed with dirty Japanese sales tactics—selling sealed packages randomly and containing one super-rare item. He was ready to steal all the fanboys' money again.

But he may have reached a point where his supereffective sales tech-niques were having negative side effects.

"You stupid son, you're spending our profits!"

"Let go, Dad! A man won't back down even when he knows he'll lose!"

"You keep throwing your money at this little girl. Who do you love more: this chick or me, your *girlfriend*?!"

"W-wait, one's like dinner and the other's like dessert, I have space for both a girlfriend and an idol…"

It looked like the fanboys had become too enamored with Rino and spent too much money, making them homewreckers.

"…Shinichi, you're not trying to destroy Tigris Kingdom, are you?" Arian asked, flashing him a cold look.

"…Sorry, looks like I took it too far," he replied, apologetic. "We've saved plenty of money, and it'd defeat the purpose if the city's people started disliking us. Maybe I'll refund them."

Shinichi went off to try to calm down the arguing people, leaving Arian and Celes in charge of sales.

All the while, Rino was sitting by the side of the stage, resting after her exhausting performance and healing spells. A little girl came running up to her.

"Rino, here. It's a letter from someone I don't know. He asked me to give it to you," she relayed as she held out a rolled piece of parchment.

"Someone you don't know?"

"Yeah, he asked me to give it to you."

"I wonder who it was."

The little girl waved and ran off, leaving Rino confused.

With nothing else to do, she looked inside, where there were symbols written in a human-world language. Rino used *Translation* to read it, and her eyes grew wide at what she saw.

"This is bad!"

My mom is very ill. She's so sick that she can't leave the house. Could you come to our house to heal her? Please come alone. If people knew about this, they'd accuse me of jumping the line.

Along with the request, there was a map with the address.

An adult would immediately have seen the note for what it was: a pathetic attempt at a trap. Even a child might be suspicious of the gaping holes in it.

But Rino was loved and protected by the most powerful creature, her father—the Demon King. She'd been raised without any malice or ill will toward her. She'd never been sullied by hate. She was pure and honest.

That's why she believed the letter and snuck off toward the location indicated on the map, slipping away so Shinichi and the others wouldn't notice.

She arrived at a narrow street crammed full of stone houses. Even at noon, she heard no sounds coming from any of them, almost as if they'd been ordered to evacuate. Rino took no notice of this strange situation, trotting up to the address in the letter and knocking on the door instead.

"Excuse me. I received your letter. I'm here," she called, and the door creaked open slowly.

Rino walked right on in, and it slammed shut behind her as soon as she stepped foot into the dimly lit house.

"Huh?!" she yelped, turning around in surprise.

As soon as she did, a number of hands stretched out from the darkness and restrained her arms and legs. She fell to the floor as her movements were completely restricted, and a beautiful young woman stepped toward her in the pitch-black room.

"Nice to meet you, Rino."

"Aren't you the Saint?" she asked, finding it in her to respond, even though she was baffled at the sight of the Saint and her holy warriors.

The corners of the Saint's mouth twitched up in a smile, smirking that Rino still hadn't realized what was happening to her.

"I warned you. Why have you not left this city?"

"Huh? What?"

"You must've known we destroyed your stage to intimidate you."

"Um, ah…"

Even though the Saint was smiling, there was something uncanny about the whole thing.

Rino was scared and troubled by this sight, but she was finally able to speak up again. "Where's your sick mother?"

"…What?"

"You said you wanted me to heal her, um, your sick mother."

The holy warriors burst into a loud guffaw upon seeing her entirely serious expression.

"Darling, that was just bait for the trap. It was all lies," offered one of them.

"Huh, what? *Really?!*" she cried. Her face was frozen in place, perplexed and shaken up.

But only for a moment: It soon melted into a relieved smile. "Ah, so your mom isn't sick."

Rino's angelic smile, a vision of pure joy and innocence—

"…She's such a saint," murmured the young holy warrior.

Those words burned away any rationality left in Sanctina.

Her face flipped from a gentle smile to a jealous scowl, as if she'd ripped off her mask to reveal the terrifying expression of a *Hannya* demon. As she leaped on top of Rino, she squeezed her hands tight around her slender neck and lifted her from the ground.

"Why? Why did you…?!"

There were no further words.

She didn't know why she hated Rino so much. Well, in truth, she probably did know, but she just didn't want to admit it, turning her eyes away from the truth.

"Lady Sanctina, that's enough!" yelled the young holy warrior, shocked by her suddenly ghastly appearance. He reached a hand out toward her shoulder.

The moment his hand entered her field of vision, she jumped back to avoid it, retreating from her position and letting Rino go.

"Cough, cough…"

Sanctina looked down with awkwardness and disgust as Rino coughed in pain. She turned to her holy men. "What should we do with her?"

"Hang her dead body from the city gates as a warning, obviously."

"No, chop her up and feed her to dogs so she can't be resurrected."

The color drained from the young holy warrior's face as he listened to his comrades casually discuss these acts of horror. "We don't have to go that far…"

"Silence!" bellowed another. "This person has interfered with our divine mission of defeating the demons. She is a heretic who's turned her back on the Goddess's will. We can't be merciful, even if she's just a child!"

"But if we do that, won't we be destroying any chance of reaching the people of Tigris?"

"Hmmm…" The overzealous holy warrior fell into silence, unable to respond to his logic.

One warrior, who'd been silent up until then, spoke up. "How about we crush her face? If it's too ugly to look at, the people will turn their backs on her, repulsed."

"Hmm, that's a good idea!"

"But you can heal injuries with magic. Is that really an appropriate punishment for a child's mischievous behavior?"

"Once she understands the weight of her sins, we could heal her injuries, and she'd understand the depth of the Goddess's forgiveness. Yes, a great idea."

"……" The young warrior had lost his words from fear.

The others nodded happily in agreement.

One of them picked up the fire poker next to the stove. "Grant my weapon cleansing holy flames, *Fire Weapon*… Lady Sanctina, as you please."

Sanctina wrapped her slender fingers around the poker, red-hot from the fire spell, and looked down at the young girl collapsed on the floor.

"N-no…," Rino stammered, trembling with fear.

For the first time in her life, she was the target of dark, twisted hatred.

She was unable to say an incantation for a spell and resist them. She tried to squirm away, but her hands and legs were still bound by magic. She soon found herself pinned against a wall with nowhere else to run.

"Why? Why would you do such a terrible thing...?"

"......" Sanctina didn't answer as she looked at Rino, who had fat tears pouring out of her eyes.

Instead Sanctina—who was feeling an odd excitement for this beautiful girl, gazing up at her and only her, this girl who'd stolen her spotlight and the admiration of others—slowly stepped closer to Rino, the fire poker in her hand, and—

"Rino!"

The door to the house was violently kicked in and the black-haired boy, Shinichi, came flying in. He didn't stop as he flung himself over Rino to protect her body, but Sanctina was tunneled in on Rino and didn't pull her hand back. With the hot rod, she struck Shinichi's shoulder instead.

"GAAAaaahh—!" As Shinichi let out a scream of agony, the foul smell of burning flesh filled the air.

"Shinichi?!" cried Rino.

"Bastard, how did he get here?!"

Another warrior tried to call to the men outside to ask what happened. Just then, the limp bodies of the lookouts were tossed into the room, bloodied beyond recognition.

The dark-skinned maid had pummeled these six skilled warriors into tattered, dirty dishrags. She stood firmly in the doorway, and her golden eyes flashed with anger as she scanned the room.

"How dare you?" Celes growled. Her frosty tone was the stark opposite of her blazing, burning eyes as she looked at Shinichi, groaning in pain, and at Rino, heaving with sobs.

Then she began to utter an incantation. "O Black Dragon, controlling the ground below, grant me a sliver of your breath, let me destroy my enemies—"

"Not that!" yelled Arian, appearing behind Celes, clamping her hand over her mouth to prevent Celes from casting a spell that was clearly dangerous.

Shinichi realized that the Saint was about to cast another attack spell at the struggling girls and shouted out to her over his pain. "Okay! We'll leave the city! We won't get in your way anymore, please stop!" he begged, bowing his forehead to the ground in apology while covering Rino's body with his own.

"You bastard! You think we'll forgive what you've done with a simple apology—"

"Hey, stop!"

With their comrades in a bloody lump, the holy warriors were blazing with heat and rage. But it was one of the more levelheaded ones that stopped them.

The maid in the doorway and the girl holding her back were both emanating enough magical power to send shivers up and down his spine. He had a feeling that if it came down to an all-out brawl, the holy warriors would be reduced to ash, unable to be resurrected, other than Saint Sanctina.

"L-Lady Sanctina, they've apologized. Perhaps we should show them the Goddess's kindness and forgive them this time," he offered, his shaky voice uncertain.

"……" Sanctina didn't respond, but she did take one final look at Rino's tearstained face, throw down the fire poker, and walk toward the door.

She didn't bother making eye contact with Arian and Celes, who were glaring at her aggressively as she passed by. The holy warriors lifted their mortally wounded companions and followed after her.

Once the sound of their footsteps had faded away, Shinichi lifted his head and hugged Rino's small trembling body again.

"I'm so sorry, Rino. It's my fault you had to go through this horrible mess."

"It's not your fault, Shinichi… Your shoulder!"

Even at a time like this, Rino was more concerned for others than herself. Shinichi felt like bursting into tears, but he let go of his tight grip on her.

Celes cast a healing spell on his shoulder, and the burn vanished without a trace.

"Just now—did His Highness see this?" he asked.

"He's unaware. After the performance, he left for his daily training."

"Oh good..."

Shinichi was relieved they'd avoided the worst possible situation. If the Demon King had seen what had just happened, he'd destroy not only the Saint but the entirety of Tigris Kingdom. "I'm so glad we made it."

When Rino slipped away from the stage, they hadn't noticed anything out of the ordinary. But some of the village children, her ardent fans, did and tailed after her because they were curious as to why.

When they trotted after her to this house and peeked in, they were scared out of their minds, sprinting away in a panic.

At around the same time, Shinichi had finally realized she was missing, and they were starting to search the area when they ran into the hysterical gang of kids. The children told them about the house, and Celes used *Fly* magic to get them there. That's when they burst in through the door.

"How can you say that? They made Lady Rino cry. I wouldn't forgive them even if they died a million deaths."

"I can't forgive them for this, either!" agreed Arian.

She'd been busy trying to rein in Celes's dangerously infernal rage, but she was mad, too. Shinichi looked at the two girls, with their eyebrows knit together in anger. He was berating himself on the inside.

"...Yeah, I guess I didn't want to do something too horrible since the enemy was a cute girl."

He definitely wouldn't call himself a feminist, but he didn't make a habit of attacking girls. He'd wanted to resolve the situation as peacefully as possible.

"But I can't show mercy to someone for making our supercute Rino cry," he muttered in a low voice, taking the smiley-face mask from his breast pocket and covering his face.

The church had its own ideas of justice. He wasn't about to denounce it all, but they'd done some pretty horrendous and unforgivable things when it came to defeating the demons: They were unconcerned with people's lives; they inflated prices to manipulate them; they were eager to burn a child's face, leaving scars on her soul that would never heal.

"I'll show them a living hell, fit for those scumbags," spat Shinichi.

Beneath his smiling mask, hidden from Rino, he wore an expression of demonic rage.

As the darkness of night draped over Tigris Kingdom, three suspicious people cornered a young man in a back alley.

"Hey kid, behave yourself. And hand over everything in your pockets."

"Yeah, you wouldn't want to end up buried in the ground, would ya?"

"Urgh…!"

At knifepoint, the young man handed over his wallet, heavy with silver coins.

If this had happened a few days ago, he would have resisted, perfectly prepared to be stabbed. He might have tried to fight, run, call for help—anything—since his injuries and death could be reversed. It would have been more important to protect his money and his pride.

In terms of the cost to heal his wounds, he could make the thieves cough up some coins to offset it once the guards had them under their care. Even if the guards didn't catch them, his neighbors and coworkers would have raised the money to have him resurrected, especially once they heard the news that he'd fought bravely against the criminals.

But the church was prohibiting any and all resurrections, not to mention the kind young girl who'd been treating the people for free had disappeared from the edges of the city four days ago. The young man couldn't win against the fear of a permanent death.

"Hah, smart decision!" jeered one of the men as he took the young man's wallet and kneed him in the stomach.

"Gah...!"

"Heh-heh-heh, that'll teach you not to wander around at night!" he taunted as all three started kicking the young man.

He was hunched over in pain as they continued to punt him. When they noticed he wasn't moving anymore, they finally walked away.

"Har-har, it seems our work has gotten so much easier lately."

"It's all thanks to the Goddess."

As they counted off the coins in the stolen wallet, all three men broke into wide, gleeful grins.

From the perspective of these muggers, the cathedral used be one of the places they avoided as much as possible, almost as much as prison. If they went to get something healed, there was a chance someone would cast *Mind Reading* or *Liar Detector* spells on them, finding out about their criminal history and leading to their arrest.

But thanks to this new ban, threats and intimidation were much more effective—as seen in the incident above. It seemed that the Goddess Elazonia herself didn't have enough foresight to imagine this would happen.

The swindlers were elated at having outmaneuvered the hated church and its followers. It was about time for them to go spend the stolen money at a brothel, when a woman's pale white arm extended from a narrow side street and beckoned them to come hither.

"Whoa?!"

Was it a ghost? The three criminals let out a little screech but realized they were wrong when they looked closer.

It was a woman wearing pure-white priestess robes. Her pale golden hair was shining in the moonlight. It was the alluring face and serene smile of the newly appointed head of the cathedral—the girl known as the Saint.

"Tsk, how'd she find out?!"

They brandished their knives, assuming she'd discovered their recent acts of violence already.

But the girl didn't cast an attack spell. Instead, she slowly pulled up the hem of her robes with an alluring smile, making them shiver with delight.

"Would you like to play with me?"

"—Huh?!" The men gulped and gaped with desire at her pale thigh, slender yet shapely and supple in all the right places.

"Heh, heh-heh-heh, I didn't know you sold services other than your healing spells."

They were being invited to sleep with her, her pure and saintly body. It was something the average citizen wouldn't have ever dreamed of doing, let alone these shifty men loitering in a dark alley. As their dreams became reality, they were excited beyond belief, disappearing into the shadows at the beckoning of her finger—

"AAAAaaaah—!"

Their cries of anguish echoed through the dark night.

It had been a few days since the troublesome lot had disappeared. But the Goddess's cathedral was still as empty was ever.

Those with life-threatening injuries continued to trek to the church, but the lightly injured and ill stopped coming in altogether, as they were unable to pay the outlandish fees. Even some of the devout believers were coming in less and less. They still had yet to hear a response from the king of Tigris Kingdom.

"What's taking so long? How long does he intend to make us wait?"

"We're not even doing resurrections. How can they sleep at night? How are they not worried…?"

The holy warriors were grumbling to one another in discontent. They didn't realize their own mistake.

It was true they'd robbed the people of their sense of security. The citizens were more aware than ever that they wouldn't be resurrected even if they died.

But they weren't going to give in so easily. After all, they'd started to view the church as their enemy. This was compounded with Rino's die-hard fans: The church had not only abused them over the years but also chased her away. They would rather be dead and buried in the ground than give in to their demands.

The other reason was that the ban on resurrection couldn't be *completely* enforced.

"Dammit, got away again," swore a holy warrior as a group of them returned to the cathedral, wounds on their foreheads, arms, and legs.

"You mean another load of dead people?"

"Yeah, I found a wagon with them hidden in the cargo…but when I tried to arrest them, some other people started throwing rocks at me, and the guys ran away, cart in tow."

His face was twisted in irritation, and the other men looked at him sympathetically as they cast their healing spells on him.

The fact of the matter was that the resurrection ban was limited to the Tigris Kingdom. That meant people could rush corpses to nearby churches and cathedrals in other towns. If they got there before the bodies decomposed, they could get them resurrected.

Obviously, Cardinal Cronklum had written to the churches nearby, instructing them not to resurrect citizens of Tigris. But while the bigger cities with a larger clergy could turn them away, smaller villages with a single bishop were a different story. With a constant lack of funds and their personal connections to the people of Tigris, the bishops couldn't deny them these services, especially if they were willing to pay.

On top of that, these bishops, considered failures in the church's eyes, had been thrown out of the big cities. They didn't exactly feel inclined to follow orders from the pompous cardinal, living in luxury at the Archbasilica.

Not that the holy warriors would understand. They'd been raised alongside the cardinal in the Archbasilica, a small world of its own.

"Anyway, doesn't this mean that Cardinal Cronklum's plan failed to bend this kingdom to the Goddess's will and defeat the demons?"

"If we'd been respectful from the beginning and asked for their cooperation, I don't think it would've come to—"

"Show some respect!" belted an older man, reprimanding the group of younger warriors for muttering on and on about their failures.

Sanctina had been watching this pointless argument in silence until now. But she seemed fed up with it all as she stood and placed her hand on the exit door.

"I'm going out for a little while."

Four holy warriors jumped up to escort her, and they walked down one of the main roads of the city.

As they passed through town, the passersby looked at Sanctina with piercing glares sharper and harder than needles.

"It's her fault that Rino…"

"Have you heard that rumor?"

"Yeah, she might look all proper and high and mighty. But she's a massive pervert."

Hushed insults and murmured rumors followed them. The holy warriors' faces clamped down into scowls, but Sanctina's face didn't budge, as if her smile was caked on her face.

Whenever she turned toward the gossiping housewives, they'd awkwardly look back and scurry off.

Whenever she made eye contact with a burly man, his cheeks flushed red, and he covered his rear for some reason as he shuffled away.

Oh, the unchosen people are so crude and annoying.

Her smile masked her true feelings toward these average, faithless, untalented, ugly commoners. It was the highest form of contempt—it was indifference.

She was the Saint, a powerful magic user chosen as a hero. These commoners should be groveling on their hands and knees and praising her. They should be rejoicing in her presence. She was their version of the Goddess Elazonia. She was superior to them. That's why she acted in a saintly way.

She'd stopped plucking flowers, killed a pitiful cub, burned a beautiful red dress. She was in alignment with their expectations, pure and beautiful. She shared her smiling face equally with all, and yet—

"...How annoying," she muttered to herself. Even the holy warriors around her couldn't hear her whispers.

Everything had gone so well up until now. She did everything the children's home caretaker had asked her to, everything the holy book had said to, everything Cronklum had ordered her to. And everyone praised and loved her for it. Why wasn't it working in this city?

"...It's that girl's fault."

She didn't blame her inexperience or naïveté or her insufficient plan for completely falling flat. She redirected her anger to that girl, burned and branded into the back of her mind.

Her long, lustrous black hair. Her gentle eyes, a red brighter and deeper than any ruby. Her small, pale hands as they cured so many with no fear of blood or disease; her smile, flashing at even the most unsavory men; her beautiful voice, ringing out like a songbird—

As these thoughts filled her, her feet subconsciously carried her to the area far from the center of town. But the girl wasn't there. Of course she wasn't.

It seemed there were plans to reinforce the city walls. A figure in a hooded robe, pulled all the way down, was writing on the ground. He looked like a surveying engineer.

Nearby, there was a young minstrel performing on his lute for a group of children.

"And the evil Demon Queen appears. With her hand, she captures the kindhearted Princess Rino."

"Don't give up, Rino!"

"You can do it, Rino!"

The children cried out in excitement. The song was a parody, narrating when Rino was kidnapped, and a criticism against Sanctina and her warriors.

"You! How dare you mock us!" boomed one of the holy warriors angrily as he ran toward them.

The group of children dispersed and dashed away in fright.

"It's the evil churchmen! If they catch you, they'll roast you alive!"

"I hope that heroes beat you up!"

"Filthy rats, watch your mouths…!"

His face was burning red with rage as he chased after the taunting children continuing to spout their insults.

In an attempt to stop him, the minstrel stood in his way and shouted. "Hey, hey, are you saying it wasn't enough to destroy my good business connection? Do you really have to get in the way of my services for children now, too?"

He was incredibly upset at losing Shinichi as his customer. They were his best clients, not just because they paid so well, but because they had given him a lot of inspiration for new music.

The holy warriors tended to dislike minstrels and people in other similar wishy-washy professions. This one turned even redder as he screamed back.

"Silence! Do you know what will happen to a beggar like you? You steal money through your vile performance art. Do you know what we'll do if you stand in our way? We're the followers of the Goddess!"

"…Hmm, so we're beggars, huh?" the minstrel replied. His fake smile—strictly for business use—was frozen on his face, and his eyes sharpened. "You should be careful insulting us… Everyone is already fed up with the church's ways and being forced to worship the Goddess."

After those final words, he headed toward the city gates as if he no longer had any use for this unhappy place.

"Hmph. Even his final words are poor. Fit for a beggar," the warrior snorted.

But the robed figure, the supposed surveying engineer, overheard their conversation, and his face paled as he prayed they'd rest in peace.

Without televisions, radios, and the Internet, the only way to get information from other countries and cities was through merchants and minstrels. In fact, there were many people who would never once set foot out of their own country in their lifetime, so the minstrel's songs told them about countries and scenery outside of their own, heroic tales, and the heart-wrenching romances of princesses. They were storytellers and musical idols—the journalists of this world, bringing news to the people. However, because their art was their livelihood, it was tough, requiring strong ties with those around them to exchange popular songs or gossip.

In other words, the holy warrior and his careless remarks had made an enemy of the media. And the media controlled this world.

There were many instances when a minstrel threatened to ruin the reputation of someone or their close friends. They all ended in the minstrels stealing their magical spears and the untimely deaths of heroic men. Not that there was any way for these holy warriors to know, much less Shinichi, of course.

"Lady Sanctina, spending any more time here will be unpleasant. Why don't we return to the cathedral?"

"Or how about we go chase down that king and harass their court for refusing to give us a reply?"

"…Sure," Sanctina replied halfheartedly and headed to the castle as suggested.

But the answer from the minister in the waiting room was the same as always.

"I do sincerely apologize, but His Highness is not in a condition to meet with you. There is no need for you to visit the castle. We will send a reply when he is available…," the minister announced, using the same congenital disease as an excuse.

But there was none of the brazenness on his face on this day. Instead, he seemed restless and upset, almost as if he didn't even know the King's whereabouts.

"What are you hiding?!" exclaimed one of the holy warriors.

"That's preposterous. I'm hiding nothing, I simply—," he replied, but before he could finish, Sanctina rose from the couch.

She looked terribly bored.

"I'm returning to the cathedral."

"But Lady Sanctina…," called one of her men with uncertainty.

She left the room and didn't offer a reply.

She'd lost all drive to act in her saintly way or fulfill her mission of defeating the Demon King. It was a task befitting her title and expected to further increase her reputation. But that didn't matter now.

The holy warriors' faces clouded over as they chased after her. She showed no energy to keep going.

"She's been acting strange lately. What exactly happened?"

"If the rumors around town are true…"

"You can't be serious! Well, I guess some things would make more sense…"

The warriors' voices wafted over to her and reached her ears, but she didn't hear their words. Her mind was filled with the face of her nemesis, even though she had succeeded in shooing her out.

"…Despicable."

She didn't know why the mere thought of Rino's smiling face filled her chest with swelling, crashing emotional waves. Her mind was so full that she forgot to flash her all-too-familiar smile and ground her teeth in frustration instead.

Just as night fell and Sanctina climbed into bed for the evening, a sudden knock came through the door.

"What is it?"

The door opened and one of the middle-aged holy warriors stepped in. He had an eerily relaxed smile on his face as he trudged into the room uninvited.

"Lady Sanctina, I've heard you're finding it difficult to control your body. I know it's quite presumptuous of me, but I've come to help with that."

"…What are you talking about?"

"There's no need to hide it. I've heard the rumors." The warrior flashed her a lewd smile.

Sanctina sighed internally when she realized that it was happening again.

Over the years, she'd flawlessly maintained a pure, virginal body—as expected of a saint. But every now and then, she would hear some baseless rumors and scandals, muttered by the men who desired her beautiful, developed body and the women who envied her.

A popular one was "the Saint is Cardinal Cronklum's mistress." Which was absolutely idiotic. Since she lived in the same home as him, she was well aware the seventy-year-old man still had women around. Not that it was something she wanted to know.

But Sanctina was his poster child. He looked at her as if she were his favorite painting, with a certain amount of appreciation, but he'd never once looked at her in the way a man looks at a woman. If Cronklum had desired her body, it wouldn't matter if he was her adoptive father or a cardinal; she'd launch her most powerful attack spell at him. The thought of a man sleeping with her, let alone touching her, disgusted her so much it made her skin crawl.

I was right. All men are scumbags driven by carnal desires.

It was the same with that young hero boy, the one who'd tried to push her down and violate her. The men of the city and the holy warriors saw nothing but her full chest and perky butt. No matter how much they tried to hide it, they just gazed at women with that lecherous look in their eyes.

Even as she spat and cursed at men in her head, she was thinking about how to get rid of this man in the most saintly way possible.

"Sanctina, release your pent up desires on me!" he cried suddenly.

Just when he'd removed his pants, he planted both hands against the wall and stuck his foul bottom in her direction.

"...What are you doing?"

This was so unexpected that, dumbfounded, she couldn't help but ask for clarification.

But the response was a meaningless, idiotic, and bewildering cry that burned away her last shred of self-control.

"Please, Sanctina, thrust your holy ☆ saber into my waiting scabbard! Ah, not realizing that you're actually a beautiful boy with exquisitely full breast augmentation was my greatest mistake!"

Sanctina could only think of one word to express that this man's greatest mistake was to exist. "...*Force.*"

The transparent hammer of energy struck his protruding rear and blew through the wall.

"Gaaah...!"

"What was that?!" cried the other holy warriors as they gathered upon hearing the sound of the crashing wall.

When they saw their comrade buried in the rubble, they were shocked and confused, especially when they noticed Sanctina, frozen in her position after casting an attack spell.

"Lady Sanctina, did you do this?"

"Why would she... Wait, is she trying to squash out those rumors?!"

"Even if that were true, how could she treat us like this...?"

They looked at her intimidatingly. Sanctina couldn't even gather the energy to explain away whatever false conclusions they were jumping to.

"...Screw it," she spat, full of resentment, before opening the window and leaping out.

"Lady Sanctina!" the holy warriors cried after her, but she ignored them and ran away down the dark city streets.

What exactly were these rumors? What had driven the holy warrior to such a ridiculous act? What was the story everyone seemed to accept as the truth? She didn't know. She had no idea. There was one thing, however, that she had absolutely no clue about.

"...What was his name again?"

She couldn't remember the name of the warrior who'd ambled into her room with a lewd look nor those of the warriors who'd helped him up.

She remembered being introduced to them before they left the Arch-basilica, but ever since then, she hadn't called them by their names even once.

It was a working relationship anyway. All the men did was stare at breasts and butts. She didn't want to bother stowing their names in the very back corners of her brain.

It wasn't surprising that someone in such a superficial relationship would believe these rumors. Doubly so if the other person didn't even bother to remember their name.

As she came to this realization, Sanctina subconsciously carried herself to the familiar streets, leading to the outskirts of the city.

But on this small deserted street, a shadowy figure stood in her way. The figure wore a jet-black cloak, melting into the shadows alongside his inky hair and leaving the white mask with an uncanny smile floating in midair. The silhouette slowly removed the mask to reveal an even more disturbing smile in the moonlight.

"Good evening, Saint. You've saved me the trouble of calling on you." The black-haired boy snickered as he crumpled a piece of paper, prepared to invite her out. "The events of this evening were quite unfortunate, ha-ha-ha."

Sanctina assumed he'd observed what had happened using *Clairvoyance*, seeing that he chuckled so happily. She was irritated by this sight and inconspicuously tried to cast an attack spell, but he seemed to predict her movements.

He pointed down a side alley. "You're interested in what kind of rumors they are, I imagine. The source of it all is right there. I invite you to take a look."

"......"

Sanctina didn't like how he talked down to her but wordlessly walked to his side and looked down the alley.

There was a lowlife of a man, collapsed on the ground with his bare bum exposed and an expression of ecstasy scribbled on his face. Her narrowed eyes snapped open in surprise as she looked at the hideous scene.

Next to the man was another figure, cheeks flushed red and brow slick with sweat—a ravishing young woman with pale-gold hair and jade-green eyes, wiping her forehead.

It was Sanctina.

Her full breasts and supple limbs were exactly the same. There was only one difference. From between her legs stood erect the vile proof of manhood.

"……" Sanctina was lost for words at the horrendous sight but quickly regained control of herself and chanted one word. "*Dispel.*"

The *Illusion* spell melted away to reveal its true form, hidden behind her fake self.

Its skin was pure white, its hair pale pink, its limbs slim but muscular. The only thing that didn't change was the foul thing between its legs. It seemed to aggressively announce it was a man. Bat wings protruded from its back, and a long black tail curled from its rear. It wasn't human.

It was an incubus.

"Aaah! I'm so embarrassed! A woman's seen me naked…!"

"What are you talking about? You're the one who's sodomized over thirty no-name criminals," accused the black-haired boy.

"It's consensual if they enjoy it in the end!"

"If you keep blabbering on, you're gonna get stabbed! Especially in a legal case of male-on-male action. You know that, right?"

The boy continued to banter, arguing that even if it was between two men, this was still a crime, but Sanctina had no interest in their exchange.

It also didn't faze her to see an incubus assault men instead of seducing women.

"So you are an agent of the Demon King," she said plainly.

"Yup. Though I'd have thought you'd have guessed by now," chuckled the black-haired boy. He shooed the incubus away and took his time to kindly explain his plan. "My goal was to prevent you from gathering magic in the conductor so that I could protect the Demon King. And we've already succeeded."

He continued, saying they'd already informed the people throughout the city that the holy warriors had destroyed the stage at her bidding, that they'd lured Rino out and attacked her, and that it was their fault Rino left the city. As revenge, he used the cross-dressing, man-loving, perverted incubus to spread rumors that Sanctina was actually a man and went around assaulting men every night.

"With the ban on resurrections, I thought a serial-killing demon would have had more of an effect, but you know."

Obviously, he'd feel too guilty about killing civilians, so he'd concocted a plan to sacrifice the criminals, specifically those who were men. That way, he didn't feel too bad, even if they did get hurt.

"By the way, I could have used a succubus, but I thought that would make you more popular with the men. Or would you have preferred that?"

"……"

Sanctina didn't reply to the crude question and glared back with cold eyes. But he didn't flinch as the corners of his mouth twitched up into a smile.

"Either way, your reputation would plummet to the ground, and no one would be willing to cooperate with you."

Even if the King of Tigris were to issue a decree, no one would go along with her plan, and the Tears of Matteral would never be filled.

"If I request assistance from the Holy See—," started Sanctina.

"I wonder which would be faster: them rushing to rescue you or the Demon King reducing the Archbasilica to ash?"

There was no way she could know if he was bluffing.

"It doesn't matter anyway. You're done for," he finished.

Even as his black eyes burned and became darker, Sanctina wasn't afraid.

She could feel some magic power in him, but it probably wasn't even one hundredth of her power. A bear isn't afraid of a roaring mouse.

What she didn't realize was that even a massive bear would rot to death from a mouse carrying the black plague.

"I'm certain after watching you these past few days—you're no saint."

Sanctina's hand, rising to throw an attack spell, faltered to a stop. "...What did you just say?"

"You know what Rino's been talking about?" he asked, ignoring her question and bringing up her nemesis. "'I hope Grandma Aban hasn't fallen again,' and 'I hope Mr. Batteo hasn't caught a cold again,' and 'I hope Carlbony and the others haven't had another cave-in at the mines,' and so on."

Her mild and tender heart was still broken as she fretted over the health of her patients.

"Do you remember the names and faces of the people you've healed?"

"......"

Sanctina's silence was an affirmation in itself. There's no way someone who didn't even remember the names of holy warriors would remember the names of the dozens of people she healed every day.

"Well, a doctor's job is to heal their patients, after all. So calling them coldhearted for forgetting their names would be a bit much."

It was inexcusable for a saint, though.

As the boy whispered, he pointed at the man collapsed on the ground after he'd been assaulted by the incubus.

"You haven't shown a shred of concern for this injured man here. In fact, you've only looked at him in disgust."

If it were Rino, upon laying her eyes on the man, she probably would have run over to him and treated him.

But Sanctina didn't do that.

The only reason she healed everyone indiscriminately was because that was expected of her as a Saint. That's why she didn't have an ounce of concern for this lewd man.

She'd done no more than play her part because she wanted to be special. She had none of the determination or unconditional love that Rino had. She was just a pretty, empty vessel. Which is why—

"You're no saint."

She'd been born and raised with the sole purpose of becoming one. It was the only reason for her life, but those words crushed it all, rejected her existence completely. It was that moment that Sanctina finally saw the black-haired boy, Shinichi, for the first time.

"*Fireball!*"

The attack spell was cast out of pure rage. Its path was easy to read. He sidestepped it easily.

"Heh-heh-heh, looks like I hit a sore spot, Fake Saint." Shinichi chuckled before turning his back to the explosion and scurrying down the twisting, turning alleyways.

"Don't you dare call me a fake!" screeched Sanctina, forgetting her saintly mannerisms and serene smile as she hounded him. "*Fireball!*"

Sanctina launched another attack toward him as he fled, but he quickly turned down an adjoining alley to avoid it, without so much as glancing back. It was almost as if he had eyes in the back of his head.

"Urgh… Seek my foe and pierce their heart, *Homing Arrow!*"

This bolt of light whizzed out of her, making a sharp turn at a side alley to intentionally chase Shinichi.

"I got him!"

She stopped to peer into the alley, sure of victory, but she saw him from behind, scrambling down, completely uninjured.

"Who's there?!"

There was no way Shinichi could have blocked that spell with what little magic power he had. That meant he had to have someone supporting him nearby.

Upon this realization, Sanctina searched around her but couldn't spot any hidden figures or a third party. If she had been more calm and collected, she could have found residual magic coming from a dark elven maid observing their battle from the rooftops. She could have guessed that she was instructing him via *Telepathy* which direction to take and protecting him with magic. She could have decided to defeat the maid first, changing her tactic. But—

"What's wrong, Fake Saint? Are you scared like the phony you are?"

"Yoooouuuuuu—!" screeched Sanctina.

There was no way for her to decide anything calmly or logically. She was consumed with clear intent to kill him.

She continued to pursue him, not realizing she was being led somewhere until they reached the stage on the outskirts of the city.

"*Huff, huff...* This is where it ends." She panted, exhausted.

She didn't have much stamina, but she smiled, knowing she would finally be able to kill Shinichi.

There's nothing stopping me now. I can use Holy Torrent...

It was the largest, mightiest spell. It couldn't be dodged or defended—except by the Demon King, of course. It would incinerate Shinichi and a large swath of his surroundings into ash.

Tactically speaking, it was the right move.

But she'd made one wrong assumption, leading to her inevitable failure. She'd forgotten that her opponent wasn't an overpoweringly strong warrior or a grand magic user. He was no more than an advisor with a fairly clever brain. That meant he'd already finished prepping the "stage" for his victory far before they even got here.

"*Fire.*"

Before Sanctina could recite the incantation for her spell, Shinichi murmured and made a gesture, as if pressing a switch. The moment he did, a number of tiny explosions blasted off, releasing a strong acrid smoke and enveloping her.

"*Cough, cough...* Such petty tricks...!"

As small particles with a chili-like sharpness coated the delicate membranes of her eyes, nose, and throat, Sanctina had tears streaming down her face. But she persisted, closing her eyes and gathering her magical power.

A person at her skill level could cast simple spells without having to recite any incantations: *Wind* and *Healing*.

But when she opened her eyes, Shinichi had disappeared, and—

"About three steps forward," came a voice, along with a sharp push to her back.

"Ack." Sanctina let out a small screech as she fell to the ground.

It was the same place where Shinichi, under the guise of a survey-ing engineer, had been measuring something around noon. If she'd realized that sooner, she might have been able to change her fate.

"*Unlock.*"

Before she could get to her feet, Shinichi cast the spell. The carefully disguised door to hell—er, well, the lid to a pitfall trap swung open, and Sanctina felt a momentary weightlessness. The ground under her disappeared, until she hit it again in the next moment.

"Ah...ack..."

Even in her state of pain and distress, she scrambled to her feet and looked up as she tried to catch her breath.

The hole was ten feet in diameter and fifteen feet deep. It wasn't as large as she had expected. She guessed it was carved out with a *Tunnel* spell, seeing that the periphery of the pit was clean. There were four wooden, window-like frames set into the walls near the top. Before she could figure out what they were for, a voice boomed down from above.

"*Unlock.*"

The wooden panels in the frames snapped open, and their contents came pouring down on Sanctina's head.

The crystals were beautiful as they refracted the moonlight into rainbows. But despite their beauty, the dwarves hated them, calling them stone leeches.

They were magic conductors. Far smaller than the Tears of Matteral, but when they were used all together, they had the capacity to rival it. They poured into the gaps of her clothing, contacting her flesh and draining her of her magic.

"Agh, aaaaaahh—!"

It sapped her of her status as someone special, the proof of her saintli-ness, her magic power, feared by man and monster alike. She struggled frantically, attempting to escape, but the mountain of crystals was large enough to bury and suffocate her. Their edges scratched at her skin as she moved, changing its hue from white to red, raw.

"Stop...no, don't steal...my..."

As magic flowed out of her, so did her physical energy. She couldn't even manage to move a single finger, preparing to suffocate to death under the heaps of magic conductors.

Just then, a single rope dropped from the mouth of the pit. Any attempt to climb it was futile, as it moved of its own accord. Perhaps under a *Bind* spell, it wrapped itself around Sanctina to gently lift her out of the pit.

"*Huff*...gack..."

She lacked the strength to stand up, and she fell on her back, painfully coughing up the crystal particles in her mouth and lungs. Shinichi towered over her, looking down at her pathetic body.

"Without any magic power to rely on, even the Saint is just a weak damsel."

Sanctina squeezed out the last of her pride to respond to his coarse words. "If you want to violate me...do whatever you like. It makes no difference..."

That's what the men were always after.

Sanctina's desperate glare declared that even if he soiled her body, her soul would never give in to him.

But Shinichi seemed to anticipate this reaction and smirked, as if to say she was wrong.

He yanked her up by the hair. "You're swine feed."

"...What?"

"You and your ugly personality are only fit to be pig feed."

"Wh-what are you saying...?"

She didn't understand. She had absolutely no idea what those words meant. She was loved by the Goddess. She was the Saint. She was more beautiful and powerful than anyone.

And you dare make that feed for livestock?

"I've stolen your magic, so you can't run now. I'll cut the tendons in your arms and legs, and I'll keep you alive with healing spells while the pigs feast on your intestines."

"Th-that's..."

"You can fix any and all wounds, isn't that right? You won't die, because you're a hero, right?"

Then I see no problems, his eyes said, glinting.

Under this gaze, Sanctina saw something she'd never seen before, felt something she'd never felt before.

Throughout her life, men had looked at her in certain ways. There was a desire to use her power, like the calculating greed that reflected in Cronklum's eyes. There was crude lust. There was hatred, an inferiority complex from older men.

But what showed in Shinichi's eyes though was none of those. It was as indifferent as someone wiping a stain from the wall, as cold as someone drowning a sewer rat in a trap. It was an emotionless desire to kill her, to eliminate the undying inconvenience—Sanctina.

"Hey, do you want to become a pig instead? Maybe that's more up your alley. There's this famous punishment in my world where they cut your arms and legs short, destroy your eyes, ears, and throat, then leave you to eat shit from the latrine. Like a pig. Fun, right?"

"Y-you…are…"

Insane is what she had wanted to say.

But her throat seized up, and not a single sound came out of it. Her teeth had started chattering uncontrollably, and she felt cold, like the blood had been drained from her entire body.

When that hero boy had tried to take advantage of her, she hadn't felt this way. She was only disgusted.

When she'd defeated her first monster, she hadn't experienced this emotion, either. She'd simply thought of how easy it had been to skewer the monster with magic. She didn't even pity the creature.

When the Demon King had deflected the *Holy Torrent*, through it all, she had held onto hope. She'd known that she would win eventually as an undying hero.

But when Sanctina searched Shinichi's face, his smile was like someone had taken all the evil of humanity and drawn it on his face. For the first time in her entire life, fear took control of her soul.

"Huff, huff..." Sanctina's breathing was heavy and strained.

Her face was pale as she started to hyperventilate.

Shinichi's expression was cold and calm as he gazed down on her, but inside, he was equally tense.

She needs to give in now. But if she doesn't...

If there was any kind of defiance remaining in her, if she believed he wouldn't do it, couldn't do it, then he'd have to—

"Please stop!" A distressed cry rang unexpectedly from behind him.

"...Rino?" He turned back and saw her.

She should have been at the Demon King's castle, but here she was, with big teardrops rolling down her face. He was frozen and bewildered as she ran up and threw her arms around his waist.

"Please stop. I don't want to see that painful look of yours anymore."

"No, Rino, I—" Shinichi tried to say.

"I'd rather go back to the demon world than have you get hurt," she declared, whimpering. She stood there with a determined look on her face, even though her cheeks were wet with tears. "Even if I can't eat yummy food ever again, even if I have to eat gross food for the rest of my life, that'll be better than letting you suffer."

"Rino..."

"I'm sorry for being so selfish. It's all my fault to begin with," she said, bowing her head and cracking a small smile as she wiped away her tears. "But even if it's just to tease me, I want you to always smile... That's the thing I want, selfishly."

Rino, you're still a kid. You can be a little bit more selfish, he'd told her in the bath.

She looked up at him now, her tears stopped, begging him with her eyes to make her wish come true this one time. Even though his heart was enveloped in darkness, Shinichi smiled and nodded in spite of himself in response to such an adorable face.

"Okay, I'll stop."

"Yay, I love you, Shinichi!" she cried.

He held his hands up, indicating his surrender. This time, tears of joy ran from her eyes as she squeezed him in a big hug again.

As he stroked her hair, Shinichi could feel the tension in his chest relax.

"Oh, that's right," she remembered suddenly.

After a moment of happiness, she let go of him and kneeled beside Sanctina, who was still bound up and on the floor.

She was bewildered beyond belief. "...Ugh."

Sanctina's entire body tensed as Rino came over. She was unsure how Rino might lash out in revenge, but Rino gently took her hand into hers.

"Pain, pain, fly away, *Full Healing*."

As light glowed in her small palms, it flowed into Sanctina's wounded body, healing her skin at the spots where the magic conductor shards scratched her.

On top of that, Rino restored her magic, pouring power into the Saint's shivering body and warming it gently.

"Why...why would you do that?!"

In her weakened state, Rino could have exacted her revenge on Sanctina for all her terrible misdeeds. Why would Rino heal her instead? Sanctina was stunned and unable to understand.

Rino smiled at her. "Because you always listen to my songs, Miss Sanctina."

As an idol, she wanted to lend her fans a helping hand.

"No, I—"

She spoke over Sanctina as she tried to deny it all. "And well, you might not believe me when I say this..." Rino blushed. "...I would be happiest if everyone could be friends."

There was no hesitation or hatred. Her smile was pure and from the heart.

When Sanctina basked under its light, she finally understood. No, she'd always understood, but she'd never admitted it. This person was completely different from her. Sanctina merely went through the motions of being a saint, but her heart was empty, lacking compassion. Nothing except inflating her ego mattered.

But Rino—Rino was tender toward everyone, regardless of whether they were human or demon or even a member of the church. Even if they regarded her as an enemy and attacked her, it didn't change her love for them.

That's what Sanctina had wanted, but it was something she didn't have.

She had envied, hated, and loved Rino for it.

"......"

Sanctina sat up without a word, and Shinichi readied himself. However, he quickly realized his fears weren't necessary any longer.

She smiled. It wasn't the fake, plastered-on one that he'd seen before. It was one she'd become so used to pushing down that she'd forgotten its very existence. It was a smile made of pure joy, one that brimmed and bubbled over her heart.

"You, you are the real saint," Sanctina declared.

Tears spilled from her eyes as she finally accepted her own feelings and hugged Rino's small frame.

"I'm so sorry for all the terrible things I've done to you. I was always so jealous of you..."

"You were jealous of me?" asked Rino.

"Of your pure heart, of course, but also of your beauty, your songs! Oh, everything, everything! I was jealous of it all...!"

Of her black glossy hair, unlike her own, which was white enough to be atop an old man's head.

Of her small, adorable little body with none of Sanctina's useless curves, which only made men ogle and leer at her.

Of her clear, energetic singing voice, something which Sanctina was prohibited from embracing as she sang hymns.

Of everything. That's why she envied her. That's why she did all those horrible things. As Sanctina continued to confess, Rino's face became a little troubled. Sanctina's shoulders heaved with her sobs, and Rino reached out to pat her on the back.

"I'm not sure I understand, Miss Sanctina. You're so beautiful and mesmerizing."

"...Huh?"

"Your hair is sparkly like the sun. And I'm jealous of your big chest, which is really cool! And the songs. How about we sing together from now on?"

"...Oh, you're so tenderhearted, through and through."

Shinichi had applied so much pressure on Sanctina, pushing her to her limit and breaking down her walls. But it was Rino's cheery smile that pierced through those cracks and brought the whole thing crumbling down, opening up her heart for the first time.

With a face full of life, Sanctina looked like a completely different person as she hugged Rino's svelte body, pressed their cheeks together, and expressed her feelings.

"Rino, my saint...I love you... I love you more than anything, more than the Goddess Elazonia."

The more you hate someone, the more you can love them. Just like that, it's possible for hate to morph into love. Shinichi felt some mixed emotions as he looked at Sanctina, whose hatred had taken a sharp turn into love.

"Well, I didn't expect Rino would be the target of her hate and affections, but I guess we did sort of achieve the goal. But—"

"Ah, um, I'm very happy, but you're making me blush...," stammered Rino to Sanctina.

"*Huff, huff...* It's so adorable how modest you are," she panted.

She was breathing heavily, releasing her pent-up desires onto Rino, who was standing there in confusion.

Shinichi had one question on his mind as he watched them. "I think she just might be a lesbian who's into little girls or something?"

"I can see that," said Celes as she leaped down from above.

So that's why my approach didn't work. Shinichi was a little disappointed but satisfied by this explanation.

"By the way, you're the one who brought Rino, aren't you?" he asked.

"Yes, I'm the one who teleported her here from the castle, but *she* is the one who said something." Celes pointed toward the former hero in her red scarf, the one who was supposed to be staying at the castle with Rino.

She hung her head like a puppy being scolded.

"Arian...," started Shinichi.

"I'm sorry! But I was scared you'd transform into something you're not..."

She'd wanted to stop him from doing that horrible thing. He hadn't wanted her or Rino to see it.

Shinichi smiled wryly as he stroked her head, tears in her eyes.

"No, I'm sorry. You saved me," he said.

"Really?! Ah-ha-ha, I'm happy to hear that..."

If she were a puppy, she would have been wagging her tail vigorously.

Even as Celes was fed up with Arian's naïveté, she spoke to Shinichi in a low voice so that Rino and the others couldn't hear them. "Did you intend to follow through with what you said earlier?"

If she hadn't given in, were you going to psychologically break Sanctina by inflicting the horrendous torture methods that you described? That's what she was asking.

Shinichi sighed deeply as if to chase away the merciless feelings in his heart, and the corners of his mouth twitched up in a smirk as he answered, "If Rino had wanted me to."

"Then you definitely wouldn't have done it!" Arian pointed out, her face shining with a bright smile.

"Indeed." Celes nodded in satisfaction. She even had the tiniest sliver of a smile on her face.

Shinichi smiled back at them, but inside, he hated himself.

I can't say the Demon King wouldn't have, though...

With the exception of Arian and other powerful opponents, the Blue

Demon King Ludabite viewed all humans as no more than writh-ing worms. The only thing that stopped the hellish fiend from doing something unconscionable was his beloved daughter, Rino. It seemed she was also the last thing keeping Shinichi from becoming an actual monster.

"I hadn't aimed for this, but…," he murmured, looking at Rino's confused face as she was trapped in Sanctina's loving embrace. "It's a yakuza technique to break someone down by intimidating them and then treating them very nicely."

"You're sickening," spat Celes.

Shinichi scratched his head but was unable to think of a comeback for her usual insult. They were interrupted by loud footsteps coming their way.

"We heard a voice over here…there!"

The footsteps belonged to ten holy warriors. It looked as if they had been worried about Sanctina after she ran from the cathedral, and they split up to look for her. They were shocked the moment they laid eyes on Shinichi's crew and pointed their halberds in their direction.

"You! What are you doing to Lady Sanctina?!"

"I'm sure they want to get revenge for that time; they plan to $%&*! and %^&$£ her!"

"…Men. Always so vulgar." Sanctina looked annoyed as the holy warriors shouted their obscene assumptions.

"Oh yeah, I forgot about them," said Shinichi.

"Would you like me to end them? They aren't even heroes," asked Celes.

"No, can't do that, it'd upset Rino," Arian reminded the maid, calm-ing her down as she spouted threats.

She was obviously still angry from the time they made Rino cry.

While the three of them debated how to react, the holy warriors had encircled them. Shinichi tapped Arian's shoulder to ask her to take them down in such a way that they wouldn't die, but another voice rang out before he could.

"Ye shall go no further!"

The shout in the strange, familiar style of speech was accompanied by a number of soldiers, who rushed out and surrounded the holy warriors.

"Wh-what is this?!" cried one of the men.

"This is absurd! Are they Tigris troops?!" shouted another, clearly shaken up by the sight of the crest on the soldiers' shields.

His guess was correct.

Following the soldiers were three figures astride horses: One was the pretending-to-not-be-bald minister that the holy warriors were well acquainted with. Another was a stern middle-aged man who appeared to be some sort of magic user. The third figure in the middle was a round, pudgy young man. He was no longer wearing his usual headband and *happi* coat, instead wrapped in a grand cloak with a golden crown on his head. He signaled with his hand, and the minister and stern magic user barked orders at the holy warriors.

"Kneel! This is His Highness of the Tigris Kingdom, our young King Sieg Fatts!"

"Fools, show your respect, kneel!"

"Ah, aaahhh!"

Under the magic user's sheer force the holy warriors fell to their knees. The captain of the Fan Club, aka King Sieg, nudged his horse closer to Shinichi, who still stood tall.

The King bowed his head slightly apologetically. "I must apologize for keeping the truth from thee, Sir Shinichi. As thou hast now heard, I am in fact the king of Tigris."

"Yeah, I know."

"How dost thou know?!" Sieg exclaimed, clearly unsettled that his grand reveal had fallen short.

Shinichi just smiled wryly and pointed to Sieg's grand stomach. "Everyone else in the city does intense physical labor. They don't have the disposable income necessary to get fat. Only a noble or son of a wealthy merchant would be able to put on weight like you."

"Hmm, to think my regal marshmallow body would one day betray me…"

"On top of that, your comments earlier implied you employed maids and private tutors. You have the leadership skills necessary to lead the fanboys. There were tons of hints, actually," he blabbed. Still, he didn't let on that he was surprised to find out. "Actually, it was around the time when you started spending dozens of gold pieces a day on Rino merchandise."

"Shhh, Sir Shinichi! Shhh!" Sieg shushed.

"…Your Highness, I would like to hear the details of that later," the minister remarked.

Turns out that money had been taken from the kingdom's coffers without permission. As the minister gripped Sieg's shoulder with a terrifying expression on his face, the portly king was quite flustered and let out a heavy groan as if enduring a terrible stomachache.

"Even with your 'long-term illness'—*cough*, your bad habits of running away and wasting money, *cough*—you would not be able to face your father now without great shame."

"'Tis thy fault for denying me any meager pocket money or freedom to leave the castle!"

"Stop with that old-fashioned speech, it's humiliating. I told you that you can be as free as you want if you simply lose weight…"

"Silence! This marshmallow body connects me to my late father!"

"Which is why I suggest you lose weight so you're not beset with illness like His late Highness. It's because of that belly that you've been unable to find a bride, even in your twenties!"

"How dare you say such things…you…baldy, you shiny-headed minister!"

"Who do you think is to blame for the loss of my glorious locks?!"

With Sieg and his minister throwing insults back and forth, it was hard to believe it was an actual conversation between a monarch and his subject. Their subordinates made no effort to stop them, however.

They just rolled their eyes, bored of what must have been a daily occurrence.

While the two continued to bicker, the stern-faced magic user dismounted his horse and approached Shinichi, bowing his head politely. "I am the Tigris Kingdom's court mage, Dritem Pinyous. I must say, that was quite the performance."

"I'm guessing that you saw everything with magic?"

The mage nodded with a smile, then indicated Celes, who was prepared to cast a spell at any moment if need be. "Though I believe that lovely lady over there could have stopped me at any moment."

"I sensed no threat from him, so I let him be. Was that wrong?" she asked.

"Nope, not a problem," Shinichi confirmed.

Based on how Sieg and the court mage were acting, the royal court didn't see them as enemies. It seemed better to be open about their actions and gain their trust than to conceal things in a slipshod manner.

But there was one question on Shinichi's mind. "So why exactly were you monitoring us?"

"'Tis obvious, we wish to ally ourselves with thy folk," Sieg admitted as he tore himself from the pointless argument with his minister.

"With our folk, huh…? When did you realize who we were?"

"Immediately. You did come shortly after the Lady Saint, upon which you did grant free healing and hinder their efforts to gather magic. Only one wouldst prosper from such a plan."

"Gotcha. Guess we weren't subtle enough."

The church might be too hardheaded and blind to see the truth, but Sieg was perceptive about what was happening in other countries. He'd been collecting information on the demons and made the connection instantly.

"Furthermore, thou holdest knowledge that no normal man should, as thou did show in our talk of cancer. Thou wast able to conceive a treatment that is secret even within the church itself. 'Twas well explained once I did realize thou dost not hail from the human world."

"Actually, that's a long story…"

Sieg couldn't have guessed Shinichi was actually a human summoned by the Demon King from another world.

"Nevertheless, I have determined your identity and power. 'Tis the result of my daily efforts to collect information."

"That said, I will not write off your expenses as an investment. Are we clear?" The minister glared angrily at Sieg as he broke out in a cold sweat once again.

"Are you sure you want to become our ally and make an enemy of the church?" Shinichi asked.

"'Tis not ideal, but we have long tired of the church's ways," Sieg confessed. This time, he barely glanced at the glares sent his way by the holy warriors. "Not all of the church are nefarious. Indeed, they do raise healers, and I have much regard for those who protect the injured and ill. Nevertheless, they hold two powers with which they control life: resurrection and the heroes. Unable am I to overlook their impudent actions."

More than anything, he couldn't forgive them for letting his father and so many others with the same disease die when they could have saved them. Shinichi looked at Sieg, who had anger in his eyes, and started to explain his theory as to why but decided against it and promptly closed his mouth.

He probably won't be convinced even if I tell him that, with too low a mortality rate, the population would explode and place a severe burden on families to care for the elderly.

It was just one of the many problems that had popped into his head when he learned that this world had resurrection magic. He wondered if the church didn't hide the cure for cancer, claiming this death was predestined, the Goddess's will, in order to combat the issue. He had no idea if he was correct. Even if he was right, it wasn't like the friends and family of those who were left to die who would forgive the church for their actions.

"That's all a part of the human story, too, isn't it…?" Shinichi murmured.

"What sayeth thou?" asked Sieg.

"No, it's nothing." Shinichi had a wry smile as he continued to wonder.

"Nevertheless, I cannot forgive the church. But the Tigris Kingdom alone is unable to stand against them. If we were to join forces with your master, dost thou believe it to be possible?"

Shinichi smiled at Sieg, who never once said the words *demons* or *Demon King*.

He answered the king's question with one of his own. "I guarantee his power. But how can you trust us so easily?"

Sieg's eyes sparkled as he nodded. "You did fend off the attack from Boar Kingdom but made no further attacks, but far more important than that, Rino's cuteness is proof enough that Sir Shinichi and your ilk are not evil."

"Yup, cuteness is justice," Shinichi agreed.

"Yes, my Saint Rino is justice," Sanctina affirmed.

"Wha-wha-whaaat?!" Rino turned bright red at everyone's adoration.

"We've spent much bribing Cardinal Snobe, and that'll all go to waste… But it angers me to be controlled by such a cruel person, one who'd allow the death of our last king," said the minister.

"The only two choices I had were bowing to the church or being persecuted, but the late king employed me and allowed me to achieve great things. I would ally with even the Evil God himself to pay off my debt to him," the mage declared.

That didn't mean the minister and mage agreed on all fronts, but their hatred toward the church and loyalty to the former king won above all else.

"Which again begs the question, wilt thou agree to an alliance with the Tigris Kingdom?" Sieg asked, dismounting his horse and extending his hand.

Shinichi looked at him and then gave Rino a small push on the back. "Rino is the daughter of the Demon King, so you should ask her."

"What?! Thou art a princess?!" cried Sieg in surprise.

"Y-yes, I am Daddy's daughter. My name is Rinoladell Krolow Petrara," she stammered, a little nervous because she wasn't used to seeing the captain of the Fan Club as the king. But she took his hand with hers to shake it in a formal introduction. "I told Miss Sanctina, too, but I would be happiest if we could all be friends."

It wasn't a handshake between a fan and his idol—it was one between a king and the Demon King's daughter. For the first time in this world, the two species were tied together in friendship.

"Oh, Rino, I'm so happy for you..." Arian beamed, sobbing uncontrollably at the moving sight, but there were some present who couldn't allow this to continue.

"Betraying the Goddess and making ties with the demons... You've made the wrong decision!" boomed one of the holy warriors.

He could no longer stand to watch. Leaping to his feet, he swung his halberd at Sieg and Rino, intending to kill them. Before he could do so, however, he was struck on the back of the head and collapsed to the ground.

"Gah...!" The warrior turned back, clutching his head in pain.

But the person he saw was neither one of Shinichi's companions nor one of the king's soldiers. It was a young holy warrior, halberd in hand.

"Have you lost your damn mind?!"

"You dare betray us and the Goddess?!"

"Betrayal... No, nothing that crazy," ruminated the young warrior. He was all smiles, even as he was surrounded on all sides by his men and their weapons. "I just realized I agree with Lady Sanctina is all—this young, pretty Rino girl is way better than that old hag of a Goddess!"

"You pervert!"

Finally, an appropriate response.

The men ganged up, trying to attack the traitor, but they were far too slow.

"Rob my enemies of their freedom, *Bind*."

Sanctina's spell invoked magical chains that writhed and wrapped around the arms and legs of all the holy warriors—other than the newly awakened pedophile. All nine of them came crashing to the ground.

"Lady Sanctina, have you lost your mind?!" asked one of them, unable to believe what was happening.

Sanctina's smile wasn't her normal empty, saintly one but one filled with all the love in her heart. "No, I've simply become aware of my love for my Saint Rino. I've finally returned to my senses."

Everyone there, except Rino, was thinking, *Yeah, no, there's actually a lot of things wrong with your head*, but none had the energy left to say anything.

"Soldiers, arrest them!" ordered Sieg.

"Yes, sir!" replied the soldiers and dragged away the holy warriors, who were completely unable to resist.

"What shall we do with them now that we have them in custody?" the king asked.

"I wouldn't want anything terrible to happen to them...," Rino murmured sadly.

Sieg gave his tummy a big slap and nodded. "Fear not, we shall persuade—brainwash—them with tales of thy wonder so they will become your friends."

"Well, one's already come around," Shinichi noted.

Were Rino's shows *that* good? It seemed that the people in the church had more than a few screws loose, even when they were called Saint that or Saint this. In truth, he was a bit concerned for them, even though they were his enemies.

While Shinichi was lost in thought, someone suddenly poked him in the shoulder from behind. He turned around and saw the incubus, who'd been hiding up until now. His wings and tail were concealed, so he appeared human.

"Could you perhaps let me help with persuading the holy warriors?" he begged, so excited to persuade them through their rears that there were practically little hearts in his eyes.

"Captain, could I ask you to allow him to help?" asked Shinichi, looking at Sieg.

"Him...? Ha-ha, Sir Shinichi, thou art truly wicked."

"Not as wicked as Your Highness," he joked, playing the part of a criminal to Sieg's perfect reenactment of a corrupt cop.

Together, they sealed the tragic fate of the holy warriors.

"Um, you really are going to do something terrible, aren't you?" Rino asked worriedly, but Shinichi flashed her a bright smile.

"Don't worry, they won't be hurt. It'll actually feel good, and they'll get to know the demons better."

"Really? That's good," breathed out Rino in relief.

It was obvious that Shinichi was deceiving her, but no one told her the much cruder truth.

"I can't imagine man on man being really good..."

"This is their punishment for scaring Lady Rino. They shall endure it one million times over," said Celes.

"A man should understand what it feels like to be a woman for once," agreed Sanctina.

The pair's harsh, unforgiving attitudes mildly frightened Shinichi, and he prayed that the poor holy warriors' souls would find peace in another world.

As the day broke and the sky slowly turned brighter, various loose ends were being tied up around the city.

The other holy warriors who'd split up to look for Sanctina elsewhere were found and arrested, the pitfall trap was filled in, and the citizens who came out upon hearing all the commotion were placated and sent on their way.

"Well, things turned out unexpectedly fine," Shinichi remarked as he sat where the stage used to be on the edges of town.

He was surprisingly okay with how it all ended.

The best outcome he'd been hoping for was to crush Sanctina's spirit, but she was so enamored with Rino that they were actually able to make her an ally. On top of that, they started building an alliance with the Tigris Kingdom. It was an incredible achievement, like scoring two hundred points on a test with a max score of one hundred.

"All thanks to your virtue, Rino."

"Virtue?" asked Rino with a quizzical expression. She didn't seem to be aware of it herself.

That purity is what makes you so charming, he thought, when Sieg walked over to them, after he'd finished tying up loose ends.

"I have a proposition that would create a flourishing friendship."

"What is it?" asked Rino.

Sieg courteously took a knee in front of her, his face more serious than they'd ever seen it. "Rinoladell Krolow Petrara, will you marry me?"

"…Huh?"

Rino wasn't the only one surprised by the sudden earnest proposal. Sieg had even dropped his strange speech patterns. Everyone there was frozen in shock.

"I, of course, can't say that this proposal has no political motives, since the marriage between human and demon would serve as a bridge between species. More than that, though, I am simply a man who has fallen deeply in love with you."

"Uh, uh, huuuuuh?!" Finally understanding Sieg's intentions, Rino panicked and glanced around at the others for help.

"A marriage proposal from a young king. It's like a fairy tale…" Arian hummed, excited as any girl would be in this situation.

"If His Highness knew, this might actually lead to the collapse of the alliance…," rumbled Celes with a concerned expression on her face.

"How dare a man ask for my Rino's hand in marriage…!" screeched Sanctina, glaring with hatred at Sieg.

Finally—

"*Huff*, ahh…" Rino took a deep breath and finally calmed down before looking in Sieg's eyes and delivering her answer. "I'm very sorry."

"Mine heart is crushed!" he wailed at being rejected outright and collapsed to the ground in tears, returning to his old speech style. "Urgh, I have known, I have always known that idols and their fans did reside in separate worlds!"

"All right, all right, shall we then return to the castle where you can explain to me where that missing gold is?" the minister asked, fed up with the young king in a hissy fit, as he pulled him to his feet.

Shinichi watched them leave, then headed toward the city gates. "Right, let's go home."

"Yep!" cheered Rino energetically with a nod as she chased after him.

Arian, Celes, and Sanctina followed.

"I'm not the one to talk, but are you sure you're okay with this?" Arian asked Sanctina.

"There's no other place for a traitor of the Goddess to go. Please allow me to accompany you." There was doubt in her mind as she answered Arian's concerns with a smile. "Besides, my church is wherever my Saint Rino is."

"I would like to inform you in advance: I shall not permit you to abuse Lady Rino in any way," warned Celes with an angry glare, but Sanctina's smile didn't fade.

"I'm well aware. Until I'm cleansed of all sin, I'll allow you to shave off my meat to feed her."

"No, that would be…"

"When Rino consumes my body with her small mouth and I am digested, we will become one. It is the most wonderf—terrifying punishment, but I promise I will undergo it as required."

"…I forgive you for your sins. Please keep the cannibalism to yourself." Even Celes was overwhelmed by the pervert with a few screws loose.

I should have just let myself become a monster, then we wouldn't have to deal with this…

Shinichi sighed to himself, a little regretful. Next to him, Rino was staring up at him, lost in thought.

The marriage between human and demon would serve as a bridge between species.

Sieg had mentioned the political reasons, but they were a little too difficult for Rino to fully comprehend. She did think it would be wonderful for a human and demon to love each other, marry, and have children.

There was this kind boy who'd been summoned for her own selfish reasons but worked hard without a single complaint, who'd made her yummy food, who'd shielded her with his own body, who'd degrade himself to keep her pure and safe.

"Ah!" Rino suddenly let out a squeak of surprise at the heavy thumping in her chest—a little uncomfortable but not entirely unpleasant.

"Rino, what's wrong?" Shinichi asked as he looked at her with concern in his eyes, but Rino just shook her head, even though she could feel her cheeks turning bright red.

"Nothing." She stretched out her hand to take his.

Shinichi squeezed her hand back, and the warmth from his large hand made her heart thump again like a beating drum. Rino didn't understand what this feeling was as it filled her chest, but she did have one thought.

"I want to eat lots and grow up."

She had a feeling she might understand it when she was at least as tall as his shoulders.

"All right, I'll make some more french fries when we get home, then," he suggested with a smile as they walked, unaware of the emotions in her heart.

A human and a demon walked side by side, holding hands—friends.

Afterword

Hello to all my Famitsu Bunko readers! This is Sakuma Sasaki, the one who hasn't been able to sleep at night, ever since I got the remake of Romancing SaGa 3 (that doesn't mean I haven't been sleeping in the morning, though).

First of all, I'd like to thank everyone for picking up this book. Thanks to your support, I was able to release this second volume. As a token of my gratitude, I'm releasing a couple of short stories on the novel site, Kakuyomu at https://kakuyomu.jp/works/1177354054882231012.

There, you can read all about how the baths came to be in the Demon King's castle and how Arian befriended the bull-headed Kalbi and the pig-headed Sirloin. I wrote a lot of stuff about what happened between the first and second novels, so please take a look if you'd like to read more about it.

Also on Kakuyomu, I uploaded a short story collaboration between myself and Kaname Aizuki, the author of *The First Thing We Did When We Got to Another World Was Check the Laws of Physics*. The short story is titled *The Dirty Laws of Physics Completely Unrelated to the Goddess's Heroes*, about how Shinichi works with the main characters of *Laws of Physics* when the Demon King summons them to their world. Read it at https://kakuyomu.jp/works/1177354054882783765.

Since *The Dirty Way* is, at its heart, a fantasy series, this story ended up with a little sprinkling of magical realism.

I also worked with Setsugetsuka, the author of *It's Another World, but I'm Just Farming Monsters* to write another short story collab titled *A Dirty Day Out With the Goddess's Hero! A Magnificent Dinner*

Party! In this story, they are suddenly taken to the world of *Farming Monsters*, where their food is delicious.

It was fun to see the contrast between their world and the disgusting dishes in *The Goddess's Heroes* world, so please check it out.

Lastly, I'd like to make an announcement: I'm currently working on the next installment of *The Dirty Way*. The main heroine of the first volume was Arian, and the second volume focused on Rino, so I wonder who will be the focus in the third...? Well, do I even need to say it?

I don't have a deadline set yet, but if all goes well, I should be able to get it to you in the fall, so please don't set your expectations too high as you wait for the next installment.

All right, well, I'm about to run out of space, so I'd like to thank the illustrator Asagi Tosaka, my editing manager Kimiko Gibu, all the people at the publishers, and everyone else who has supported me. Well, that's it from me for now!

Sakuma Sasaki, May 2017

Afterword

Hello! Asagi Tosaka here.

I'm so happy Volume 2 is here! I didn't think there'd be an idol story arc in the mix...!

This time around, Rino played a really active part in the story, so she had so many outfits and hairstyles. It was really fun to draw her out of her normal design.

And the character design for the newest character, the Saint, is one of my personal favorites. I guess I'm putting my interests and tastes on full display, though...!

Anyway, thanks for sticking around until the end! I hope we'll get to meet again soon...!

Asagi Tosaka